Married to a Boss, Pregnant by my Ex

Lock Down Publications and Ca$h Presents

Married to a Boss, Pregnant by my Ex
A Novel by *Destiny Skai & Chris Green*

Destiny Skai & Chris Green

Lock Down Publications
P.O. Box 870494
Mesquite, Tx 75187

Visit our website
www.lockdownpublications.com

First Edition March 2019
Printed in the United States of America

Lock Down Publications
Like our page on Facebook: Lock Down Publications @
www.facebook.com/lockdownpublications.ldp
Cover design and layout by: **Dynasty Cover Me**
Book interior design by: **Shawn Walker**
Edited by: **Lashonda Johnson**

Stay Connected with Us!

Text **LOCKDOWN** to 22828 to stay up-to-date with new releases, sneak peeks, contests and more...

Acknowledgements

We would like to thank our readers for their undying love and support. Without you we wouldn't be where we are today. This collaboration is nothing short of amazing and you will not be disappointed because all of you deserve nothing but the best. Our future is looking mighty bright since the Gangstress and Gangsta of LDP has joined forces with two very creative pens. Enjoy!

Sincerely,

Destiny & Chris

Destiny Skai & Chris Green

Chapter 1

Storm rocked back and forth, and tears streamed down her face, as *'Never Gonna Let You Go'* by *Blackstreet* played on the iPod at her elbow, causing pangs of heartache to almost bend her over at the waist.

"Never gonna let you go away. You belong to me and I'm never gonna let you go. Never gonna let you go away. We were meant to be in love, love."

A few years ago, those words whispered from Gotti's beautiful, sexy lips setting Storm's mind, body, and soul on fire. He was her first and only, and her heart had been exclusively his. His touch drove her crazy, and when he dreamed, she dreamed right along with him. But now it was over, Storm was done and there would be no going back. He had shattered her heart and destroyed the trust she had for him forever.

The thought alone made her tears flow down her cheeks harder, like a waterfall, as she wrote her final letter to her ex-boyfriend. Storm reminisced back to when they were teenagers and he would sing this song to her all the time. She'd listen to it on repeat every night at bedtime. Gotti was away doing a three-year bid for aggravated assault and some other bullshit ass charges.

Dear Gotti,

I hope that when you receive this letter, you are in the best of health. I also hope that you understand everything I'm about to tell you. From the time we met, I've been in love with you. I've always dreamed of getting married and having your babies. It hurts me to the core knowing that will never happen. There's no need to explain what happened because you know exactly what you did, and I hope it was worth it. The sad thing is, I was ready to ride the full bid with you. I didn't care if I had to wait three years, thirty years or three hundred years. I would've been there until the clock of life ran out of time. No sentence was too much when it came to you.

Gotti, you hurt me so bad, words can't express the pain I'm in as I write this letter listening to our favorite song. Our bond was strong, and I can't believe you ruined it. I swear I hate you, right now and I never want to see you ever again in life. Just know that I will never forgive you and that's on everything I love. So, here goes—I am leaving you and going on with my life. All the years we've spent together were everything to me. I never thought I could ever walk away from you, but I want you to hurt the way I'm hurting.

I want you to spend your days and nights in that cold cell crying and thinking about me. I want you to wake up in cold sweats and lose sleep on a daily basis. If you commit suicide after this letter, I wouldn't feel no type of way. That's how much I despise you, right now. I also want you to know that I'm getting married to a wonderful man. One that loves and appreciates me, and is loyal and faithful to me. If it wasn't for him picking up the pieces of my shattered heart and putting it back together. I don't know where I would be.

I'm grateful that he came into my life and showed me what true love is. You took my virginity, but he'll be my second and only until death do us apart. I'm very happy where I am, I just want you to know this before you hear about it in there. This is best for both of us. So, please don't fight with me over this and do not try to contact me because this is the end of us forever. I wish you the best and just know that I will always love you. You were my first and I will always remember you. Please let me go!

Goodbye,
Storm

The sound of the alarm being disarmed made Storm jump up and toss all of her belongings into her bag. Then she slid it underneath the bed and did the one-hundred-yard dash to the bathroom to wash her face. When she looked into the mirror her eyes were bloodshot red. Storm pulled open the medicine cabinet and grabbed the Visine. She held her head back, squeezed a few drops in each eye and followed up with a few blinks to make sure she got every corner. After she was done, she wiped her face for the last time and went to greet her king.

Dominic was standing in the living room looking through the mail when Storm walked in. He dropped a bag on the sofa next to them. "Hello, my king. How was your day?" Seeing his handsome face always made her smile.

Dominic stood at six-feet-two-inches tall, with brown-skin, deep waves and a full beard. "My day was good, but it gets better when I come home to, my queen." His baritone voice sent chills down her spine without him laying a hand on her.

The business attire he wore definitely played a role in his deliciousness. Storm stood there eyeing her man dressed in a three-piece suit and a pair of brown Ferragamo dress shoes. Dominic was a Kingpin, running the entire state of Georgia. He tossed the mail onto the coffee table, then extended his arms out to her and pulled her close, slipping her some tongue. Storm closed her eyes and clenched her legs together in an effort to stop the juices from flowing, but it didn't help. Dominic's lips were soft and sweet. She could kiss him forever, but in order to keep her from having an orgasm right where she stood, she pulled back.

"Whoo!" She exhaled and fanned herself. "Baby please stop before you make me go back on my word." Storm laughed and wiped her bottom lip with her finger.

"I'm sorry, but I couldn't help myself. You shouldn't be so damn sexy. Good thing I only have to wait two more weeks before we walk down the aisle, then off to the honeymoon." He smacked her on the ass.

After her ex went to jail, she closed down shop, engaging in celibacy. It was her promise to him that she would not let another man explore places that were only meant for Gotti. When she met Dominic, she told him she wasn't having sex until she was married and surprisingly, he was okay with her decision.

"Are you hungry, baby? Cause I made your favorite." Storm took pride in taking care of him and having his dinner ready when he came home.

"Of course, I am, I saved my appetite just for you. But before we do anything else take that bag."

Storm picked the bag up from the sofa using her left hand. "What's in here?"

"That's fifty grand for you. Go to the mall and pick up some things for the honeymoon and anything else you can think of."

She unzipped the bag and took a peek inside. Shaking her head, she closed it and handed it to him. "No baby, I can't take this."

Dominic placed his hands inside his pocket. "No, it's for you baby. You deserve that and so much more. I just want to give you the world on a silver platter."

Those words hit her right where it hurt, in the heart and the tears began to well up in her eyes. "All I want is you, so you don't have to keep dropping bags of money on me. You just gave me money last week and I still have some left."

"Storm, just let me spoil you, please. Is that too much for a man to ask of his woman?" He looked at her closely and observed a few tears present. "Why are you crying?"

"You're everything I want and more. I don't care about what you have and what you can give me. All I want is your loyalty and for you to be faithful to me."

"Storm, baby come here." He embraced his woman, hugging her tight and rubbing her back.

Storm was standing on her tippy toes, with her head buried in his chest, weeping helplessly. "I don't know what's wrong with me."

"You're the only woman I want and that's a fact. They don't make them like you anymore. I'm a lucky ass man, I would never jeopardize what we have. I love you too much for that."

"I love you, too," she replied softly.

Chapter 2

Dominic cruised smoothly down the street in his black Porsche Cayenne GTS. His mind was only focused on the paper that it was time to pick up. Business was moving as usual, and great business only meant one thing, more money. He reached out for the volume button, turned up the stereo and let *Rick Ross* bump through the speakers.

"Shorty so fine, pussy so fresh, diced pineapples damn my baby taste the best. I nearly lost my mind."

While Dominic mumbled along with the song, he couldn't help but think about Storm. Nothing could make him happier than seeing her smile. He knew for a fact that taking the next step forward with their relationship would bring them a closer bond. The attraction and feelings were undeniable. Plus, the love was genuine.

He replaced his thoughts when he pulled inside the two-story home. He cut off the engine, honked his horn twice and sat back. While he observed his surroundings. A medium-built, dark-skinned man emerged from the house. The great duffle bag he carried, pulled heavy on his right arm. Getting to the car, he got in the front seat and placed the bag in the back.

"So, what's good, Bossman," Juve asked looking over at Dominic.

"How much is it?"

"Come on, bro, we already talked about that. I'ma reimburse you soon as the next shipment come through."

"Juve, it's been three weeks. I give you weight to sell, not to run around and spend freely because you feel that you have it. If I'm losing money, then my business ain't moving correctly."

Juve's hands begin to become tense sitting in the passenger seat. He knew Dominic was ruthless when it came down to his paper. The thought of telling him, he was dipping his nose in the product was definitely out of the question.

"Listen, Dominic, I've been working for you a long time. We're like family, all I'm asking you to do is give me a little time and let me work it off. Things ain't always going to be good, but you know I'll get this shit right."

"Nigga we shall wait. This is a grown man's business. It's no such thing as fuck ups. Now if you feel that you are underqualified to help operate this movement. I can easily replace you with someone who can."

"Dominic everything I—"

"Get the Fuck outta my car, Juve," Dominic said calmly as he rubbed his hand through his waves.

Juve held his tongue while he looked over at him with a still face. Nodding his head, he climbed out of the car and headed back for the house. Dominic cranked up the car, pulled out slowly and headed to the next destination directly down the street. No matter what happened, he always tried to keep his anger under control when it came to dealing with the same people he was feeding. One thing for sure was that in the next few months he'd have enough paper to take care of him and Storm for the rest of their lives. It was about maintaining more than anything.

He adjusted his Versace frames riding through the Cobb County city limits. Making a right turn, he pulled inside the McDonald's drive-thru.

"Welcome to McDonald's what ya' trying to order?" The man said through the intercom box.

"I need a couple of birds. What's good with that?"

"Pull around to the booth, bro."

Moving the whip around the building, he stopped when the man opened the small window. "What's good, big homie, why you just didn't pull around from the jump?"

"I'm making my presence known. How ya paper looking?" Dominic replied with a serious face.

The man reached beneath the register, grabbed the thick legal envelope and passed it to him.

"Where does this put us at now, Clyde?"

"We at five, Bossman."

Checking the time on his gold Rolex, he looked at Clyde with a raised eyebrow. "First of all, we at ten. I've never had any problem with mathematics in school. I'm going to tell you the same thing I told Juve. If you feel it's too hard to do this, let me know. I got love for y'all boys, but my money gone get made regardless. I'm just lending a hand."

The loud car horn that started to beep made Clyde spazz out. "Bitch just go around to the other window!"

Dominic shook his head looking in his rearview mirror. "If you wanna be part of this tighten up. I'll be at you soon."

Clyde nodded his head after putting his headset back on. Dominic pulled off slowly and rolled up his window. Pulling out into the street, he decided to go ahead and make his way to the house. It was late in the afternoon and riding around with one-hundred and fifty grand was surely out of the question. Thinking about how far he came, he couldn't help but smile. His hands were inside the investments of three restaurants. His connect only blessed him with the purest cocaine. When he fed it to the streets, the money began to come back even quicker. Coming up from the mud was hard, but it was guaranteed something he would never forget.

***

Tier Program, Smith State Prison

The banging on the cell door made Gotti jump up out of the bed. "Yo' why the fuck are you slapping on my shit like you crazy, pussy ass nigga."

The guard looked at him with a blank expression. "Calm down asshole it's chow time."

Opening the door the officer handed him the tray and closed it. Gotti stared at the cold meat patty and vegetables while he sat on the bed. Picking up his spoon he took a bite of the cold mashed potatoes. The sound of the envelope sliding through the crack of the door made his head rise. It had been forever since he seen any mail. Three months ago he was transferred from his current prison for the stabbing of an inmate. He ended up beating his free world charge but was shipped because of his close security.

Standing up off his bed, he walked to the door and grabbed the letter. Seeing Storm's name made his heart skip a beat. He could even smell the scent of her favorite perfume. They weren't on the best of terms, but the pain inside refused to let her go. Sitting back down, he ripped open the paper and began to read. He couldn't help but smile at her precise and beautiful handwriting.

Gotti continued to read slowly making his smile turn to a frown. His hands began to sweat as he started to clench down on his jaw slightly. He read every word until he got to the bottom and balled it up, then threw it across the room. Picking up the tray he slammed it across the door. Out of all people, he never thought she would turn her back on him. The thought of her being with another man made his skin crawl with rage.

Gotti knew she would eventually find out about all his dirty deeds he left in the streets but running off with another man was like a knife to the chest. A small smile crossed his face as he sat back down. In his head Storm wasn't going anywhere. No matter where she tried to go. He knew she could be found. The thought of trying to give his love away made him furious. Regardless of what she was thinking, it was only going one way.

Chapter 3

Storm stood in front of the full-length mirror giving herself a once over, after changing twice. She guessed three times was a charm. Loving the way, the *Fashion Nova* jeans hugged her hips, she did a full twirl and laughed out loud in excitement.

"Storm you are all that and some."

Admiring her newly found shape, she stuck her butt out and wiggled it a bit. Her body was banging and her ass was sculpted to perfection. All compliments went to her personal trainer who worked the dog shit out of her five days a week. To make sure she was perfect for her wedding day. Hard work really did pay off.

Storm applied some lipstick to her full lips, which complimented her smooth chocolate skin and almond-shaped eyes. Her naturally curly hair was cut into a Mohawk. Satisfied with her appearance, she grabbed her bag from the bed and slipped on her Gucci shades, then headed out the door to go handle her business.

She popped the locks on her brand-new Mercedes Benz GLE 350, climbed inside and put on her seatbelt. Dominic always laughed about her need to feel safe at all times. She could hear his voice in her head as if he was right there with her.

"I'm your protector and I'll always make sure that I keep you safe."

Just the thought of him alone put a smile on her face. After she was tucked in securely, she turned on the stereo then backed out of the driveway. Living a lavish lifestyle was never on Storm's to do list. All she wanted was to be comfortable and not live in the struggle. All of that changed when she met her future husband. He had done nothing but lace her with the best of everything against her wishes. The money and street fame that came along with her man meant nothing to her. She would still want him if he worked a regular nine to five.

Storm turned onto Peter Street in downtown Atlanta and made her way to the Escobar lounge to meet up with her girls, Kendra, Tia and Jade, who were also her Matron of honor and bridesmaids. On the inside, the girls were already seated, awaiting her arrival, in their private area with royal blue sofas.

Storm walked between the blue rope that separated them from the crowd and greeted her girls. "Hey y'all."

Making her way around she gave every one of her girls a kiss on the cheek and a hug.

"I thought you got lost or finally decided to give that man some ass," Kendra, her Matron of honor and best friend for over twenty years, joked. "I did the honors of getting you a fishbowl."

Storm sat beside Kendra, placed her bag between her feet and pulled her drink close. "No, girl we have only two more weeks. We can make it."

"I don't see how cause, Dominic, is fine. Ain't no way I could lay next to him every night and not throw this pussy on him." Kendra laughed and took a sip of her fishbowl.

"I know that's right cause with his reputation and good looks, he could've hit it on the first night," Jade, one of her bridesmaids agreed.

"Girl, who you wouldn't let hit on the first night." Storm threw a lot of shade in her response and her girls peeped it.

"Shit." Kendra spit out some of her drink because she already knew what time it was. She picked up a napkin and dabbed her lips to get off the remnants of the alcohol.

"Bihhh, I'm dead," Tia, the other bridesmaid, who she'd met in college at Clark Atlanta University said.

"That was shade, but it's cool. I wasn't aware that you was keeping tabs on my pussy." Jade didn't like the way she was being put on blast. Although Storm was speaking the truth.

"Trust and believe I'm not keeping tabs on who you fuckin' and suckin' as long as it ain't my man," Storm snapped and took a sip of her drink.

"Girl bye!" Jade flipped her off. "I don't want nobody you got or had for that matter."

"I seriously doubt that sis." Storm was ready to battle because she had so much to get off her chest and Jade was begging to get her feelings hurt in the worst way.

"I don't know what your problem is, but maybe you need some dick or something to calm your shady ass down. It's obvious you backed up and miserable. I'm a real bitch, I don't play games." From there it was gloves off for Storm. The moment she had anticipated from the time she got the news. The way she cut her eyes at Jade could've slit that bitch throat from ear to ear.

"Well since you wanna go there let me ask you one question, we'll see what type of bitch you really are. Did you fuck, Gotti?" At that very moment, everyone at the table was in complete silence for the first time. It seemed as if the entire lounge was quiet. Jade swallowed her spit. It wasn't like she was sippin' on shit that would keep her from responding. Storm folded her arms and waited for an answer.

Jade's eyes were sad and it looked as if she wanted to cry, but she was trying to keep it in. The words hadn't been spoken yet, but her silence was confirmation that the accusations were true.

"I can't hear you, though." She needed her to respond about sleeping with her ex-boyfriend ASAP.

Jade's mouth opened slowly. "Storm, I'm so sorry. That was never supposed to happen between us."

Tia frowned and looked over at Jade. Everything about her facial expression said she was disappointed in her. "Jade, no you didn't?"

"What are you sorry for—sorry that I found out?" Storm knew that it was true because her source was a reliable one. Hearing Jade admit it was icing on the cake. "I just need to know when it happened and how many times?"

"It only happened once, the night Deon jumped on me and threw me out of the car." Jade was in tears while she tried to justify her actions while reliving a damn near fatal ass whooping. "When you told him to give me a ride home because you were tired. He was giving me advice and one thing just led to another. I swear it never happened again after that."

Storm shook her head, as she recalled that night.

She and Gotti were at home enjoying a night of Netflix and chill when there was a knock on the door. Jade was standing there with a wet face, a busted lip and nose, a ripped t-shirt and her arms were bleeding. Apparently, Deon had accused her of cheating and beat her ass, right before pushing her out of a moving vehicle. She refused to go to the hospital, so Storm helped her get cleaned up and gave her fresh clothing so that her mother wouldn't interrogate her ass to death.

"And that was one time too many. It should've never happened. I trusted you with everything! I helped you and you stabbed me in the back like that." Storm's blood was boiling and the only thing that would make her happy right now was slapping the taste out of that bitch's mouth for betraying her like that.

Kendra and Tia remained silent, allowing Storm to get everything off her chest so she could move on with her life.

"I know and I feel bad, it was an accident." Jade sobbed while wiping her face with a napkin. "Storm if I could take it back, I would."

"Don't give me that if I could bullshit. That's what every guilty nigga and bitch say." Tears welled up in Storm's eyes. "I was the one who was there for you when Deon blew the rent money and you were about to get evicted. Cut your lights on when your dumb ass was sitting in the dark. Gave you rides because he was out in the streets riding out your gas and not picking you up from that bum ass customer service job." Storm patted her chest. "I did that because that's what a real friend does when her friend is in need. Even if she's too stupid to realize that she deserves more than that."

"Storm we can get past this, let me make it up to you! Please forgive me," she pleaded.

"I think not." Storm shook her head. "That won't be a good idea because I swear if I ever catch you with my husband. I will kill you and I put that on everything I love!"

"I wouldn't do that to you again, I promise!"

"You, won't get the chance. I don't trust you and I never will." Storm took a long pull from her straw and picked up her fishbowl while eyeing Jade. "You got me so fucked up, right now. I ought to throw this glass in your face bitch! But I'ma let you have that and that nothing ass nigga." Storm grabbed her purse and rose to her feet. "As a matter of fact our friendship is over, don't call me, text, E-mail or message me through social media. Delete my number and pretend like I never existed."

"Storm don't leave." Kendra grabbed her arm. "This is our ladies night. Sit back down and finish your drink."

"Yeah, please stay," Tia begged.

"If I stay here, I'ma catch a case and I don't want to lose my job. So, it's best that I leave." Storm walked off, but stopped and went back to the table.

Kendra smiled. "You changed your mind?"

"No." Looking Jade dead in the eyes she said, "And you're no longer in my wedding. So, save yourself the embarrassment and don't show up."

Jade cried harder and watched her best friend of ten years walk out her life for good.

***

Storm made her way inside the house slamming the door behind her. The anger was pouring out of her skin as she walked pass Dominic on the living room couch. Sensing the tension, he made his way up the steps behind her to the master bedroom.

"Hey beautiful, is everything, okay?"

"Yeah, everything is fine," Storm's response was dry as the Sahara Desert.

Dominic walked inside the room and posted himself in front of her so he could look into her eyes. "Then why are you so tense? I could see the anger in you downstairs. Did something happen?"

Her heart rate began to rise as she looked into his handsome face. The love he showed was beyond caring, it was past special. Storm could tell from his expression that her man was worried.

She planted a soft kiss on his lips and shook her head. "It was just a little dispute between me and Jade. The way I been feeling lately. I'm really done with the whole friend thing. It's a lot that comes with petty females and I refuse to have that around us."

Dominic took her hand, led her over to the bed and sat down beside her. Then placed her leg into his lap, removed her shoes and begin gently massaging her feet.

"I know sometimes you may think a lot of stuff should be different. Friends argue about the pettiest things that you can think of. It's all a part of being friends. Regardless of disputes, after the smoke clears your friend should still be there. If they aren't, that means you made a bad decision on who you allowed to enter that space. I have friends, but I keep things discreet to ensure my business is handled. If I don't make the line you can never cross it," Dominic said with a sincere tone.

Storm couldn't help but think on his words. It was damn near like he was reading her mind. Unfortunately, the line for Jade had been crossed and there was no understanding allowed in the damn picture.

"Baby, friends don't betray friends. There shouldn't be such a thing as a line when it comes to someone you have respect and love for. If something happens to turn things sour, then it obviously wasn't a friendship from the jump," she pleaded her case.

Dominic continued to rub her feet as she released her steam. From the sound of her voice, he could tell she was hurt about something.

"Storm we will be married real soon. My mission is to make you as happy as humanly possible. I've been setting a lot of things up to make sure we can sit back for the rest of our lives. This isn't the time for any altercations. Whatever you feel should happen that is what we will do."

"I know everything will be okay. We're just going to focus on our wedding and us. The rest of the trash means nothing," Storm replied wanting to change the subject by giving him a warm light kiss. She sat back as he flashed her a bright smile.

"That's how I like to hear you talk. I got a few things that I have to handle today so I may be a little busy. I've been thinking a lot."

She was curious. "What are you thinking about?"

"Giving this life up and passing it down to someone trustworthy enough to hold the position. I can never leave the game because this life is what made me. But this is a way I can play the backfield and still accumulate this money.

"Dominic I already told you before, I respect the man you are. Money doesn't have any significance to the love I hold for you. I'm okay just the way we are." Her words were sincere. "And that's understandable baby, but the sun doesn't shine forever. When it's all over I want to be able to say we don't need or want for anything. There's never enough money that I can spend on you. Your price and worth are way above any number I can count. You're going to be my wife. So, let me handle this job as your husband to make sure me and my lady are good. You know I can never disappoint you."

Just the sound of his voice and words started to tingle the inside of her panties. Even the look in his eyes made her want to climb on top of him. It was nothing better than having the warm, secured love of a real boss.

He rubbed his fingers along the side of her face and placed a soft peck on her forehead.

"What makes you love me the way you do?" Storm asked, ready to rip her clothes off and break their agreement.

"It's not hard to understand, my queen, it's just you. Most people spend their entire life searching for the one to be with. When all you have to do is follow your heart. No solid couple in this world made it without taking a chance. After that, it's up to the two to see how long that chance will stick around."

Blowing her a kiss, he walked out of the room leaving her alone. Storm's thoughts ran wild as she laid back on the bed and began to ponder on her feelings. Life for her was great, but things were just beyond difficult. However, there was one thing she was focused on and it wasn't falling down.

Destiny Skai & Chris Green

Chapter 4

It was late that night, around 9:30 pm to be precise when Dominic made his way to the dealership. The meeting with Jacob was long overdue and the closing of the contract had to be handled. Slowing his car down at the light, he made the turn onto Piedmont Road. He pulled inside the lot, drove past the luxury vehicles and parked in front of the main entrance. Then he stepped out, closed his car door and headed into the building. Making his way to the large office, he powered down his cell phone before he stepped in the meeting.

"I'll have to call you back at a later time tomorrow," Jacob said, watching Dominic enter, then hung up the receiver. He then picked up the single sheet of paper and slid it across the table. "Those are the finishing documents to close out the rest of the deal. It's a sixty-eight-thirty-two split. That's twelve percent for the manufacturers, twenty percent for me and the rest will be sent to whatever bank account you would like me to put on file for you."

Dominic pulled the gold tip pen from his pocket while he read over the paper. A smile formed across his face while placing his signature on the dotted line. "I'm glad you were able to pull the strings to get this handled, bro. I'm thinking about going all out with this investing game. I have another meeting tomorrow about opening the proper account to hold the new funds I will be receiving."

"Listen, Dominic," he folded his hands and placed them on top of the desk. "You've placed your money in my hands on more than one occasion and I always bring you back a profit. You're the reason my daughter's college education is fully paid for. I need to be the one thanking you."

"Our tab is at ten, Jacob," he responded, while pulling the two zips of cocaine from his pocket, then pushing them across the table.

"La-La fucking, Bamba. Is this the same thing from last week?" Jacob replied with a huge grin.

Nodding his head, Dominic stood up and headed for the door. "I'll be in contact, Jacob."

"And I'll be ready with every penny."

Making his way out of the dealership, he took a look at all the cars he'd be getting a piece of. The money he was flipping would double, which would make him invest even more. The profit from the drugs was only a bonus. The only thing left was letting the business run and keep accumulating more paper. Everything he wanted in his world was coming true and there was no such thing as losing.

* * *

Clyde nodded his head to the music that played on the radio as he made his way down the street. Dominic had just blessed the game on the re-up of product and the streets were calling loud for the paper to be made. Driving past the Old Hickory Lake Apartments, the car radio cut off the music, as the foreign number popped on the dash.

He turned the volume up and answered. "Yo', who dis?"

"Nigga it's me."

"Oh shit. What the fuck goin' on, cuzzo? Why you calling me from this weird ass number, nigga?" Clyde said.

"I'm using somebody else's line. These people came through today."

"And what did they say?"

"They set a date for the fifteenth."

"What? Bro, that's in like two weeks."

"Yeah, I know, I gotta lot of shit to handle. I need your help on a couple of jugs to get back on my feet. I gotta pay a bunch of muthafuckas a visit. I'm on some real money missions."

"Listen, bro, just chill. You know I'm in the mix with a real boss plug. All you got to do is come eat and I'ma feed you this shit.

"Say less, bro. I gotta go, but you know what's going on now. Just keep that on the low."

"Man, I got you, nigga. What are cousins for?"

"Bet!"

Clicking the end button, he smiled at all the good news that was coming back to back. It was a fact when the next shipment dropped, money was about to flow.

Chapter 5

"I love you, Beautiful," Dominic said through the phone. Hearing him say those words always made her heart melt. She couldn't wait to walk down the aisle with her king.

"I love you too, Baby." The biggest smile spread across her lips, as she sashayed down the hallway.

"Well, you have a good day. I'll see you later on tonight for dinner. Just name the place, I'll meet you there after work."

"Yes, my love I can do that. You have a good day as well, be safe."

"Always baby," he responded before hanging up.

Monday morning rolled around quickly and it was back to work for Storm. Unlocking the door to her office, she stepped inside, flicked on the lights, then closed the door behind her. Despite the fact, that she loved her job, she knew it was going to be a long day. Storm worked as a human resource manager at Grady hospital ever since she graduated college with honors. It had been her lifelong dream to work in the medical field. Since it had become a reality, she loved every minute of it.

Dominic wanted her to quit, but she couldn't let go of it so easily. It took hard work and dedication to reach her goal and it felt damn good to live it out. Storm walked over to her desk, pulled open the drawer and placed her belongings inside, then she plopped down in her big comfy leather chair.

"Storm," she sighed. "Today is going to be a good day despite the bullshit in your life. You are getting married to a wonderful man, so fuck, Gotti and Jade."

No matter how much she tried to give herself a pep talk and convince herself she didn't care. That pain ran deep, and it hurt like hell. Eventually, she'd have to put on her big girl panties, build a bridge and get over it if she wanted to have the perfect marriage. The wedding was twelve days away, she needed to pull it together quick fast and in a hurry. There was no way she could walk into her new marriage with old bottled up feelings toward her ex. In order to get over it, she needed to go through it and cry herself a river away from home. Music always had a way of helping her cope and face her emotions head on.

So, she opened up the Pandora app, the first song that played was *Keyshia Cole's Trust and Believe*. Looking up at the ceiling she shook her head.

"God, I see you being funny, right now." She laughed, trying to make light of the situation, but all it did was make her cry while singing along. *"You pushed me far, you brought me to this. You had my heart but then you blew it, and I'm so over you. So, get lost, boy. Who do you think that you are?"*

Her lightly applied foundation was now ruined, as it made a light stream down her cheeks. She dug through her top drawer, found some napkins she collected from the cafeteria and wiped her face.

"So much for being cute."

All those years she invested in Gotti went down the drain right along with her friendship to that bitch, Jade. To think she was actually holding him down during his bid. Thinking they were going to be together forever. Life had a funny way of throwing a monkey wrench in your plans. Saying think again *bitch,* ain't no happy ending. There was a knock on the door that interrupted her thoughts and pity party.

"Give me just a minute!" she shouted, trying to get herself together for the first problem of the day.

Before she could make sure she was intact the door swung open and in walked Kendra. "Hey, Boo," she screeched, closing the door behind her. "You just getting in?"

"Yes," Storm replied, putting away her mirror.

Kendra walked over and stood on the opposite side of her desk. "I called you yesterday, you didn't call me back. What's up with that?" She slid her hands inside of her scrub pockets.

"I know, I'm sorry. I just needed some time to think." Storm powered on her computer, avoiding eye contact and pretended to be busy in hopes that she'd leave.

"I guess girl." The music caught her attention and she bent down just a little to see her face. "Why you playing this sad ass song?" Kendra paused for a brief second while coming to her senses. "Storm are you, okay?"

"I'm fine." She lied.

If Kendra didn't know anyone else like a book, she knew her girl. She could sense there was indeed a problem. However, getting her to confess was like pulling teeth. But she wasn't leaving until they talked about what was bothering her. She removed her hands from her pockets, walked over to Storm, placed her arms around her and rubbed her back.

"You can talk to me with no judgment, you know that."

Storm sobbed into the arms of the one person she knew she could trust without a shadow of a doubt. In her presence or behind her back, Kendra was a thoroughbred female and very loyal. No matter what went down, she could trust her with her deepest darkest secrets.

Without a second thought, she blurted out, "I still love Gotti and I'm hurt by what he did to me!"

"I know you do."

Storm stopped crying and lifted her head from her shoulder, looking Kendra in the eyes. It was obvious she was surprised by her response. "Does that make me a bad person?"

"No." She picked up the napkin from the desk and wiped Storm's face. "You invested a lot of time into that relationship. And both of them muthafuckas are nasty as hell for crossing that line. However, don't allow that to affect what you are building with, Dominic." Kendra threw the napkin in the trash and sat down on the desk.

"I'm not. I love, Dominic—*I am in love with him*! There's a difference. I would never jeopardize my relationship with him for, Gotti."

Kendra nodded her head. "Good because he is a Godsend. I love him like a blood brother. You deserve happiness and so does he. The two of you were meant for one another."

"Thanks Ken, that means so much to me. That's why I love you." Storm was finally able to smile.

"You're welcome, Boo. That's what best friends are for. To pick up the pieces when these no good ass men can't act right." She smiled back and winked. "Fake ass friends, too."

"You got that right." Talking to Kendra had her feeling much better. So, she was ready to start her day. "I really needed to get that off my chest and now I can get to work."

Kendra hopped off the desk laughing. "Yeah, just use me for my comforting words, then kick me out your raggedy ass office."

"It's all love, Boo." Storm giggled.

"So, you're good now?"

"Yes, I promise."

"Good. And whenever you get into a little funk just remember that people come into our lives for a reason or a season. Next Saturday you will be marrying the finest bachelor in all of Atlanta and you will live happily ever after."

"I will do just that," Storm replied.

Kendra looked at the watch on her wrist. "Well, I gotta go. I have patients that I need to comfort. You know, make sure they make a peaceful transition into the afterlife." She was a registered nurse in the hospice department.

"Well go and save some lives, I'll see you at lunch."

"Take it easy and think about the right man." Kendra walked over to the door and let herself out, so she could start her day.

Confessing her feelings about Gotti was exactly what she needed. It released those crazy thoughts from her mind, body, and soul. Now she was ready to start her new life with the man of her dreams.

* * *

It was late in the evening and a slight breeze blew swiftly in the area as Dominic pushed his Porsche Cayenne 957 through the streets of Atlanta. The music played at a low tone as his mind shifted to his future wife. Her beauty and brilliance was all a blessing from above and a prized possession to have within one person's hand. For Dominic, it took a lot of women to make his world float. After Storm came into the picture that same world felt as if it was a bubble lifting into the sky. The flawless eyes and natural hair, she was all the woman a man could ask for. Her loyalty was another factor on why he sold

30

his eyes her bondage. It was hard to come across a beautiful black woman without an outstanding background for drama and deceit. Storm happened to be the complete opposite with more qualities. On first sight, he knew she was a keeper and not just that, but a friend for life.

Growing up many of his past relationships were quickly migrated to the trash can. Or caused bad blood to spill over in jealousy and the evil four-letter word they call love. Dominic promised himself that keeping his grind tight would always come first. But gaining a little more age and wisdom caused his mind and heart to search for more.

He pulled into the next intersecting lane and made the right heading down to the soulful street of Albany Avenue. He observed the small eateries and poetic groups that bundled around each other to hear the fly speeches of poem legends. He couldn't help but smile. His taste was far different from the average young street hustler who understood nothing but ignorance. His style was more of a classic gentleman that adored peace with a passion. Without a heart you are only a man without direction, one that was bound for destruction. Even though his life was part of the fast lane. It was actually time to pump the brakes and begin his new future.

Turning inside the small lot of cars, he parked and stepped out. Dominic's six-foot frame was draped in a dark grey Armani suit. The Salvatore Ferragamo dress shoes added a plus to his taste as he walked with confidence towards the entrance. As he made his way into the restaurant a smooth crisp sound of a saxophone blew humbly. The medium sized crowd snapped their fingers in unison for the next poet who made his way up to the small stage area. Turning his head, he spotted her at a nearby table. Her soft finger snapped along with the crowd as he moved closer without being noticed.

"Now what's a beautiful woman like yourself doing sitting alone?" he asked with a charming smile.

Dominic looked down at Storm and her heart slowly melted while looking up into his eyes.

"I'm waiting for, my husband," she responded in a sexy tone while crossing her legs.

The white Dolce & Gabbana lace fitted dress that hugged her firm booty demanded all his attention. Not to mention her naturally curly hair that she wore in a Mohawk that he adored so much.

"Well, I'm glad I got here first." He teased before planting a delicate kiss on her lips.

The Jazz Bar and Grill began to grow quiet as the lights dimmed for the next speaker. He slid in the chair next to Storm. He grabbed her hand giving it a gentle squeeze while watching the performer step to the microphone.

"This is a project, I recently wrote entitled, Temptation," the man spoke in a peaceful tone before the melody tune spread throughout the room. "Temptation—temptation is the reason we can never understand patience. That black cloud over your mind that rains on your brain to make you neglect waiting. I've never fully understood how we could be put on this creation, just to tear down walls of our African History and rewrite civilization. This is more like chemicals and gases that fuels respiration. Taking so much oxygen from the pure that they need resuscitation.

"Hmm—and I never thought a simple conversation could change a bad situation. Or thoughts of someone hating, but I'll give you time to think of what I'm saying while I'm patiently waiting. As I'm breezing through obstacles moving the way through my life shoes. I'm wondering why bad luck in my life runs fluently and I still choose to break rules. The smoke that fills my lungs occasionally helps me come to the conclusion that the commitment to this horrible lifestyle will only lose. I refuse to let the mother who births me into existence watch the news to see her youngest flower, who she bloomed become a tragedy of a six by nine cell or a tomb."

"These are just the basics of being a man and getting yourself to a certain groom. It's kind of simple, like when you were younger trying to balance food on a spoon. So, go ahead black soul I'll be sitting here patiently waiting for a circle of sins to come back around just for temptation."

The eruptions of finger snaps filled the room as the talented young speaker made his way off the stage.

32

"I've never heard anything like that in my life. How did you find this place?" Storm asked with an intrigued gaze.

"Growing up peace and music placed me into a comfortable spot. I searched for a place that could grant me more of that feeling and landed here. I hope you are enjoying the new atmosphere. Instead of our usual wine and dine. You know I was going to come and pick you up from work. So, we could arrive together, but a little business call came up," Dominic announced before waving a waiter down.

"Yes, sir, can I help you?"

"Could you bring me a nice cold bottle of Moet and Chandon, please? And keep the extra for yourself," he replied, sliding the crispy c-notes across the table.

"Right away, sir! Will you lovely couple be ordering anything off the menu tonight?"

"We should have it figured out by the time you get back."

Nodding his head, the man disappeared into the mist of the bar to retrieve Dominic's request.

"So, is there any chance I can find out what your day has been like?" He asked as she gazed around at the large painting portraits that clung to the walls.

Sighing, her mood changed before answering his question. The usual kind of sluggish behavior. "I talked to Kendra throughout the day to pass time. But mainly focused on having a wonderful dinner with you."

"What do you think about quitting your job?"

"Quit? Dominic, I can't just up and quit my job baby. I mean I love what I do. Why would you want me to stop working?"

"Because I'm going to take care of you forever. I want you to travel the world with me. I've put in some extra work to see that we already have four businesses up and running within two months. We're not going to be hurting for anything. If I say, I'm ready to be your husband that comes with the responsibilities and obligations. I told you once before there is no price that is equal to you."

Dominic spoke in a humble tone while looking deeply into her eyes. Matching his gaze, butterflies fluttered through her stomach.

From his assuring demeanor, she knew his words were golden including his heart.

"Sorry for the delay on your champagne, sir," the waiter interrupted by placing it on the table with two glasses. "Are you ready to order your meal?"

She gave Dominic a smile, picked up the menu and begin reading. It took approximately thirty minutes of different conversations and several rounds of wine before the meal arrived at their table. After sharing dinner and a few more laughs. They came to the realization that the Moet was starting to throw a little kickback. They made their way to the front of the bar. Dominic paid the tab and headed to the car with Storm wrapped closely in his left arm.

"I want you to know that I love you," he said helping her climb into the driver seat.

"I love you too, Dominic." She leaned over and planted a soft kiss on his lips and smiled.

"I'm going to follow you."

"Okay." She started the engine, adjusted the radio notches to the R&B station and waited for Dominic to get in his truck before pulling off.

* * *

They walked through the front door of their home. Storm made her way upstairs to the master bedroom. She kicked off her heels, grabbed a pillow and flopped gently down on the bed.

"I take it, you had a good time tonight?" Dominic asked taking a seat beside her.

"Yes, it was very unique. Nothing like I expected it to be, but I enjoyed every second of it."

"All I want to do is make you smile and experience wonderful, new things with you. I promise you'll understand more after you're declared that married woman," he uttered while rubbing a hand across the bottom of her back in a pleasant manner.

The tingle and throb that sparked through her love button caused her to sit up just inches away from his face. "I don't have a doubt in my mind about you being the best husband ever. It's a very big step and sometimes it scares me," Storm replied truthfully.

Staring at her with love and sincerity, Dominic grabbed the back of her neck and placed his tongue inside her mouth. The space between her legs instantly melted as he took every inch of her breath away. His masculine hands massaged the side of her cheeks. The sins could be felt trying to creep out of her skin. The sensation, the urge. Storm's mind was so stressed and under pressure that her body needed the strong feeling of his touch so badly. As their tongues locked and intertwined in heavy desire. Her hand wrapped around the back of his head. Suddenly a quick flash of Gotti's face sparked through her mind causing her to jump back from his grasp.

Storm caught her breath before speaking. "I think I need to get in the shower and get ready for work tomorrow."

Dominic lowered his head and thought for a few moments before placing a peck on her cheek. Then he whispered softly in her ear. "I can't wait to make you mine."

Storm watched him walk out the door and started feeling guilty. She knew shaking those bad emotions were going to be tougher than she thought.

Chapter 6

Storm sat at her desk processing new hire packets when there was a knock at the door. She glanced at the clock and realized it was lunchtime. "Come in," she shouted.

In walked Kendra with a huge smile on her face. "Girl get off that computer. Do you see what time it is?"

"Yeah, I just looked and I'm ready." Storm stacked the folders on top of one another and grabbed her purse from the drawer. "Let's go because I am starving."

"Good." Kendra walked towards the door with Storm on her heels. "So, how was dinner last night?"

Storm closed her office door and both women proceeded down the hall. "Girl, it was everything. We went to this Jazz Bar and Grill, where artists showcased their poetry."

"Sounds interesting and fun." Kendra smiled at the way her best friends eyes lit up whenever she spoke about Dominic. Then did a little dance with her tongue sticking out. "Ooh, did y'all get drunk and have nasty sex afterward?"

Storm knew that topic was coming again. She laughed it off and tried to play it cool. "Yes, we got drunk, but we didn't have sex." She took a deep breath and glanced at Kendra. "We were very close to going back on our agreement."

Kendra grabbed Storm's arm, forcing her to stop walking. "Hold up. So, you mean to tell me that the two of you were drunk and horny and did absolutely nothing?"

"Unfortunately, yes." Storm sighed in frustration. "And I wanted to have sex so bad, but I couldn't do it."

"Why not?"

They continued their journey outside of the hospital where they were met by the afternoon sun. Storm covered her eyes with her shades and purposely ignored the question. "Who's driving me or you?"

"You, duh. Now, tell me why you couldn't have sex with that fine ass man." Kendra wasn't giving up until she got an answer.

"It's too embarrassing, I can't."

"Girl, you better tell me, we don't keep secrets." Kendra stopped and frowned her face. "Don't tell me he has a shrimp?"

Storm shook her head laughing. "Hell no! My man is definitely blessed in that department."

"So, what's the damn problem because I'm confused?"

"Okay—" Storm paused for a second. She knew she could trust Kendra without a shadow of a doubt, but what she was about to say sounded crazy. Even in her own mind, so she knew what her friend was about to say. "This is what happened. When we got home, we were drunk. So, of course, four play came into the equation. It was so intoxicating, in my mind I was like fuck what I said since we're getting married in less than two weeks anyway. So, we both get completely naked, then Gotti's face popped up, snatching me clean out of the mood."

"What—are you serious?" Kendra couldn't believe the bullshit she was hearing. "You, let a nigga that don't matter stop you from sleeping with your husband? Come on, Storm, seriously!"

"Yes, I did." Storm dropped her head a little. When the scenario rolled off her tongue, she recognized how silly the excuse sounded. "Ken, you don't understand. It was like Gotti was staring into my eyes saying I could never get rid of him."

"Storm—" She grabbed her hand. "—I do understand. We've endured your pain together. I'm telling you now not to let him ruin the best thing that has happened to you. Dominic, is beyond perfect. You can't get better than what you have."

"I know sis, thanks."

Storm and Kendra hugged.

"You're welcome. Now, let's go eat because for the last time I am starving."

Storm approached her vehicle and saw something white flying from underneath the windshield wiper. "I know damn well this is not a ticket."

She unlocked the doors so Kendra could get in and went to retrieve the paper. When she pulled it and got a good look at it her hands trembled in confusion. Storm immediately looked around the parking lot to see if she noticed anything out of the ordinary. When nothing seemed out of place she climbed into her SUV and started the engine.

"What's wrong with you—they gave you a ticket?" Kendra was concerned once she saw the frantic look in her friend's eyes.

"No, but I wish it was a ticket instead." She held up the envelope. "It's a letter from, Gotti."

"What the fuck?" Kendra was baffled because according to their calculations he had more time. "Is he out?"

"I don't know." Storm ripped the envelope open and pulled out the letter, so she could read it out loud.

Dear Storm,

I received your little threatening letter and let me just say that it was cute. I ain't gon' lie, you had me pissed off, but I shook that shit off quick. You must be crazy and out your goddamn mind, if you think I'm going to let you go that easily. That will never happen and I will never stop looking for you. So, you can get that out of your head. You belong to me, you need to remember that. I'm laughing, right now because you really thought I was gon' let you break up with me and leave me in this world alone. I don't think so, you know better than that. Me and you were meant to be and soon enough, I will be gracing you with my presence. So, tell that nigga it's over because I'm taking what's mine and that's on Big Mama's head.

You know you hurt a nigga to the core with all that bullshit you said. But I know you ain't thinking straight, so I'ma let that slide. I may have loosened your leash, but I never let it go and I'm not letting go either. All I'm gon' say is watch yourself and don't get too comfortable. Because I'm gon' reappear when you least expect it. I was your first and I will be the last. I love you more than life itself, so let that sink in. If I can't have you no one will. Romeo and Juliet baby!

Love your man, Gotti

Kendra's mouth was agape until she read the last words. "Storm, what the fuck did you do to that nigga? Prison made him crazy as hell I see."

"This is just Gotti's way of trying to get me back. I wrote him a letter a while back letting him know, I knew about him and Jade. I also mentioned, I was getting married and for him to move on with his life."

"I don't know Storm that letter sounds like a threat if you ask me. Are you going to tell, Dominic?"

"No." Storm ripped up the letter and envelope so she could trash it. "I'm not about to have him worrying about me and another man. Gotti had his chance and he blew it. I'm with Dominic and I'm happy."

"Don't you think you should give him a warning before the destruction occurs?" Kendra huffed.

"He's in prison. What can he do from there?" Storm pulled out her phone and searched the web for the Department of Corrections website.

"I'll show you in a minute."

A quick search revealed what she already knew. Gotti was still incarcerated. She handed the phone to Kendra so she could see for herself.

"See he's locked up and he will be there for a while longer. By the time he gets out he won't think to look in my direction."

Kendra handed the phone back. "So, you think the letter is fake?"

"No, this is definitely his handwriting." Storm scratched her head. "I just don't know who would've put it on my truck."

"See and that's what frightens me. You need to tell him so he can protect you. Maybe get you an escort to work or some shit. Hell, he could bring you himself or you can ride with me."

"Kendra, relax, I'm going to be okay."

Storm backed the truck out of the parking spot and headed to the nearest restaurant to grab a bite to eat.

* * *

After Storm left work for the day her mind was in shambles, so she stopped by the liquor store to get a bottle of Belaire Rose. It just didn't make sense of how she would get a letter from Gotti in the first place. To receive it on the hood of her vehicle was fishy, but to have her work address on it was downright disturbing. On her way home, she thought of a million ways it could've happened and only one name stayed in heavy rotation and that was Jade.

"That conniving, bitch!" Storm shouted and hit the steering wheel, blowing the horn in the process.

The second she pulled into her driveway, she whipped out her cell and dialed the backstabbing bitch's number.

Jade answered like she had been waiting on her call. "Hey, Storm. How are you?"

"Miss me with the phony ass introduction and tell me why the fuck would you give Gotti my work address? And why did you feel the need to put that shit on my windshield?"

Jade looked at the receiver like Storm had completely lost her mind. "Storm, I don't know what you're talking about. I swear!"

"Bitch, I don't believe shit from your lying ass mouth. I know you've been talking to him and told him where I work. How else would he know?"

"It wasn't me. Why would I tell him that?"

"Oh, I could think of a few reasons why, but that's not important, right now. Just tell me why you did it."

Jade pleaded with tears in her eyes. She knew when she came across her next hard time Storm would not be there to help her like she'd always done in the past. "I wouldn't do that to you. I've hurt you already and all I want is a chance to repair our friendship."

"I've told you already we will never be friends again. So, get that out of your head."

Storm ended the call, turned off the ignition and got out of the vehicle. Dominic wasn't home yet, so that gave her time to unwind and put her emotions in check before he got there. The first thing she did upon entering her domain was kick off her heels and toss her purse onto the black and white contemporary sofa set that she loved so much. When Dominic surprised her with the house she took pride with decorating their palace to make sure it was fit for a king.

The home had five bedrooms and four bathrooms, which she planned on filling with kids the moment they went on their honeymoon. Storm wanted kids, but Dominic never expressed any real interest in them. Nor did he dismiss the fact. Storm sauntered into the kitchen with the bottle in her hand and placed it on the black marble island. She then pulled a wine glass from the cabinet and rinsed it out. Dropping some ice into the glass, she poured the alcohol to the rim and took a long sip like it was water.

"Damn, I needed that." She sat the glass on the counter and walked to the fridge so she could get dinner started.

Storm had been home for two hours by the time she heard Dominic set the alarm on his truck. Dinner was done and she was on her fourth glass. The Rose` definitely had her buzzed, but she wasn't drunk. An instant replay of the other night is not what she was trying to face once again.

Dominic walked into the kitchen looking dapper as usual in his three-piece suit carrying his bricfcasc. When he saw her face he immediately lit up. Coming home to his queen was the highlight of his day.

"It smells good in here, baby. What did you whip up for your man?" He licked his lips and placed his briefcase on the counter.

Storm met him halfway to greet him with a wet kiss to his lips. "I made you some lobster pasta, salad, and red lobster biscuits."

"Damn, that sounds good. See you know the way to my heart is through my stomach."

"That I know." Storm twirled on her heels in a half circle and walked to the stove. "Come sample it."

Dominic's eyes were stuck on her ass, as he walked up and hugged her from behind. "I would love to sample this."

Storm giggled. "We're almost to the finish line and you can have all of this whenever you get ready."

"You got that right."

She picked up a fork and twirled it in the pot, then turned to face him. "Open your mouth."

Dominic did like he was told, allowing Storm to feed him. He chewed a few times before swallowing it. "That's banging, baby."

"I'll fix our plates while you wash up."

"Okay." Dominic grabbed her wine glass and took a sip before sitting it back down. "How much have you had to drink?"

"Hmm, about four glasses." Storm looked at him with the googly eyes. The same way she did when they first met. Since then her feelings had grown stronger with each passing day.

"Be cautious cause I'm telling you now I ain't stopping if we go too far tonight." Dominic winked at her before walking out the kitchen.

Storm leaned against the counter and sighed. "Oh, how I would love to cross that line tonight. I am in desperate need of love and affection."

By the time Dominic made it back the table was set, soft music played in the background and Storm was waiting beside his chair. "Have a seat my king."

"That's okay baby you have a seat."

"You always take such good care of me. So, allow me to take care of you for a change." He was hesitant at first, but he went ahead and sat down just to make her happy.

Storm grabbed a cloth napkin and placed it on his lap.

"Thank you, baby," he replied.

"You're welcome." She then sashayed to the other end of the table and took her seat.

Dominic blessed the food before they both dug in. The sound of Teddy Pendergrass filled the room while the couple ate in silence. When he was done with his food, he pushed his plate away and wiped his mouth.

"I need to talk to you about something." Dominic took a sip from his wine glass.

"Okay, I'm listening." Storm sat her fork down on her plate and gave him her undivided attention.

"The wedding is almost here and I think you and Jade need to have a sit down to hash out your differences. Everything is already in place and we can't be short on bridesmaids."

Storm tooted her lips up in utter disgust. "I don't want her at my wedding or sharing the happiest day of my life. That day is reserved for people that have my best interest at heart."

"Baby, come on now. Are you sure you're not making this bigger than it needs to be? The two of you have been friends for years and I think you can get past whatever happened. Good friends are hard to come by."

"I know that and I no longer consider her a friend."

Dominic had a strong feeling that Storm wasn't going to change her mind, but he had to try once more. He sat up and looked deep into her brown eyes.

"How about this, allow her to be a part of the wedding and afterward you never have to speak to her again if that's what you really want to do."

Storm shook her head side to side a few times before she finally replied, "That's not a good idea."

"Storm let's not ruin our perfect day with the pettiness of a cat fight. That's not who you are. Do it for me, baby, please."

Dominic never asked Storm for anything, so for her to hear him ask for someone else's forgiveness spoke volumes about his character. However, due to the circumstances Storm found that request impossible to fulfill. But she didn't want to be selfish or just flat out say no, although that *was* what she wanted to do.

Instead, she decided to give him false hope. "I'll think about it, but I can't promise you anything."

"Please consider it, that's all I ask." Dominic got up from the table and tossed the cloth onto his plate. "I'm going to take a shower."

When Dominic walked off Storm downed her glass and quickly fell into a sunken place. He had no idea how much heartache Jade had caused and for him to want her in attendance crushed her to the core. Just the thought of seeing her face after finding that letter earlier would guarantee Jade, a fresh ass whooping. Storm rested her head on the table and closed her eyes to think for a moment.

Chapter 7

Glancing at the time on his Audemars Piguet watch, Dominic pushed the new white Range Rover Dynamic through the sunny city. Thanks to his close friend Jacob he'd be able to snag the latest rides before they touched the car lot. Making the investment was one of the best decisions he'd made in a while. If you weren't hustling to increase your dollars. You were grinding to waste it. It was his objective to pursue the absolute best for Storm and in order for that plan to prosper all troubles in an eyeshot view had to be straightened.

He pulled into the Longhorn Steak House, parked the SUV and stepped out. Then slid on his Persol sunglasses. He smoothed out his white button down before tossing on the purse blue jacket of his Tom Ford two-piece. As he headed towards the entrance, he made his way inside and gave the waitress a bright smile as he approached.

"Hello, sir. Are you dining alone today?" she asked with seductive eyes as his Calvin Klein cologne pumped through her nostrils.

"No, actually I have a friend who's already waiting for me. I'll just find her table if that's okay," he replied while quickly checking his phone.

"Sure," she mumbled pathetically, feeling that her luck had shifted for a change.

As he walked through the aisles. He scanned the restaurant until he spotted Jade's hand in the air. "Hey, I hope it wasn't too much asking you to meet me here. It was kind of a late notice thing," Dominic spoke as he arrived at the table.

"It's fine, no big deal," she replied.

After calling the server over to order the small lunch. Dominic felt his phone vibrate. As Storm's name flash across the screen, he hesitated but let the call pass due to the mission at hand.

"As you know the wedding is approaching fast. Have you gotten the chance to speak with Storm about the bridesmaid dresses?" He asked trying to ignite the conversation.

Jade's facial expression spoke volumes about the situation. Her aura completely switched, and it was obvious Storm's name added tense to the mood. "No, I still haven't spoken to her about that. Things are kind of difficult, right now, and I don't want to make the situation worse than it already is."

"Worse?" He paused for a second. "Listen, ever since I came into Storm's life I've always trusted her to be a woman of her word. And I've also witnessed a bond with you and the rest of her friends that's unbreakable. There shouldn't be anything that you girls can't talk about and come to a resolution like sisters do all the time.

"Can I ask you something, Dominic?"

"Sure," he responded right before the waiter approached their table and sat down the two meals.

Jade waited until he departed before she finished her question. "If one of your boys ever did anything hurtful to you would forgiving him be an option in order to save the friendship?"

"It depends on what he did. A lot of things happen between people all the time. Sometimes a veil could be placed over one's heart because of what another feels about what occurred. You also have situations that could be worked out even though the heart is sour about the issue."

"What if one of them lied or cheated with, Storm? Could you forgive that?

Dominic nearly choked on a piece of steak after hearing that comment. Sitting down his fork, he wiped his mouth with the cloth napkin. "No one would ever be that close to do something like that from the start. A lie is something I could brush off but cheating with my wife could create a never-ending problem."

While listening to his reply, Jade couldn't help but lower her head and take a bite of the salad. The slime ass guilt was weighing heavy and it was clear that she was swimming a little too deep.

Dominic raised a brow then crossed his fingers while sitting up straight. "What exactly are you and, Storm, beefing about?"

"That's my girl and I would never try to hurt her intentionally. What happened between me and, Gotti, was an accident," Jade expressed with regret on her face.

"*Gotti*," he repeated confused. That name was certainly foreign to him.

Jade realized she'd just dug a deeper hole. She uttered the first thing that came to mind. "I have to use the ladies' room."

"Not until we finish this conversation," he stated with authority in his tone. "You mind filling me in on what's really going on?"

Jade eased back down in the seat. His stare sent jitters through her body. "I know, I'm not perfect. When I wake up it kills me not to hear from her. She's like the sister I've never had and regardless of how much I apologize, she's not gonna forgive me."

"Explain."

Silence loomed for a second before she eventually released the secret of her deceiving actions. "Before you and Storm got with each other, I slept with her ex-boyfriend, Gotti. It was just a one night stand. Something that was never supposed to occur. A couple of weeks ago it just so happened to come out and she's been furious with me ever since," Jade admitted nearly in tears.

Dominic couldn't help but ponder on the statement he was just told. It was definitely hard to forgive and forget, but it was even harder to build a relationship with a person and call them a friend. Even if Jade was wrong it was a subject that his mind couldn't grasp. Storm had never informed him of this Gotti person, which made it kind of hard to deal with the problem at hand.

"So, you're telling me this is the reason, Storm, is vexed?" He questioned her to see if there was anything else she was concealing.

"Yes."

"In that case you are wrong and I'ma have to side with my lady on this. Crossing lines with someone you truly care for could easily tear away a good relationship. Being a friend means you have to contribute the same loyalty that's given. That's what balances everything out, Jade. Now, if your feelings are artificial, I can guarantee it, will show. Even though you hurt Storm, I honestly feel you are sorry. Just make sure you're on time for the wedding and I will talk to her."

"No! Please don't say anything about this to her. Don't you understand? If you do this, she'll know I told you and she's gonna beat my ass."

Sensing her fear, Dominic nodded with the assurance that the conversation would be concealed. He surely didn't need Storm thinking he was running around behind her back. In his head, the immature cat fighting was something they could eventually come around to letting go. At least long enough for her to attend the wedding.

"I'll arrange for you to pick the dress up tomorrow. You're gonna presume your place at the ceremony and let me worry about, Storm."

Placing a crispy Ben Frank on the table, Dominic stood to his feet. "I suggest you form the best apology possible. The only thing I can do is try to help, but I refuse to force her to accept disloyalty."

As she watched him depart, Jade knew something was bound to go terribly wrong. All she could do was hope for Storm's mercy when it was time to cross that thin bridge.

Once Dominic made it back outside, his phone rang just as he climbed inside his vehicle. "Clyde, you know this is an off day," he answered while starting the engine.

All that was on his mind was Storm. This was certainly an awkward problem between two friends, but definitely understandable. The only thing that piqued his interest was her being frustrated about a person who was no longer a factor. It only showed him that he needed to put more effort into making her happy.

"What's good, big homie? I'm ready for you to come pick that up whenever you're free."

"Maybe, later on, I'm handling something at the moment."

"Understood, I needed to run something by you. Also, I got a cousin who's on his way home. I know how you are about meeting new people, but I also know he can meet your standards with the business. He's not the average nigga and I know you need a true soldier if something was to ever get a little ugly," Clyde mentioned.

"Remember, you can't vouch for somebody who I've never met. That would be something I'll have to decide for myself."

"True." Clyde nodded his head. "All I can say is I would never bring the drama your way. Just giving you something to think about."

Taking his request into consideration. He sat quietly. "Bring him to me whenever he shows up and we will go from there," Dominic replied before ending the call.

New members of the team wasn't actually a bad idea. It was time to finish the last few runs to the money and call it quits for good, Dominic thought before leaving out of the parking lot.

Chapter 8
One week later

The day Storm had waited for all her life finally presented itself. She was about to walk down the aisle and marry the man of her dreams. All of the heartbreaks and dead-end relationship with Gotti was all worth it in the end. Being that she'd found her true king. After being incredibly anxious for the past few weeks, her nerves had a sudden shift. That feeling had turned into full-blown nervousness.

As Storm stood in the center of the room, she fanned herself while Kendra dabbed her forehead with a cloth. "You need to relax before you mess up your makeup. Then you'll be walking down the aisle looking like the *Bride of Chucky* instead of *Cinderella*."

Tia burst out in laughter. "Or Bridezilla."

Storm rolled her eyes and pouted. "Shut up, Tia. That's not funny, I'm a nervous wreck. What if I'm not cut out to be anyone's wife? What if this marriage changes the dynamics of our perfect relationship?"

Kendra grabbed both of Storm's arms. "Stop it! You're going to be just fine. You are good enough for, Dominic, and that's why he asked you to marry him. He's the type of man that's very selective and he chose you for a very good reason. Stop beating yourself up, if anyone deserves happiness, Storm, it's you."

Storm seemed to relax a bit after her best friend gave her the reassurance she needed. She took several deep breaths. "Thanks, Ken, I really needed to hear that."

"That's why I'm the Matron of Honor." She winked. "Besides he has to love you if y'all getting married and he ain't hit that yet."

"Period," Tia chimed in.

"Oh, my God!" Storm screeched. "Ken what if the sex is bad? What am I supposed to do?"

"Well, Sister Mary Clarence, you on your own with that one and you stuck like, Chuck. No one told you to become a nun all of a sudden." She turned Storm around so she could look in the mirror. "That should be the least of your worries look at this fabulous dress."

"You gone have to teach his ass, but I seriously doubt that's necessary with, Dominic. That nigga looks like he'll tear the lining outta some coochie. Break a bitch's pelvis! Girl, you better have a few drinks in case that man kill you, cause I know he backed up like a muthafucka."

"Tia," Kendra shouted. "Girl, we in a church did you forget that?"

"The Lord knows my heart and besides he knows I play all day." Tia giggled.

Storm stood in front of the mirror mesmerized by her fitted Berta Balilti Illusion Sleeve Embroidered Trumpet Gown. The white lace was perfect against her brown skin. At that moment, she knew for a fact her hard work and dedication to the gym had paid off tremendously. The dress fit perfectly. Her hair was up in a high bun with a crystal headpiece. A true Queen at best.

"Wow!" Storm gasped. "I'm really getting married y'all! This is so bizarre."

Tia was finally done getting her makeup done. So, she got up from the chair and stood next to Storm. "On a serious note sis, you deserve all the happiness in the world."

"I do, but I feel like something bad is going to happen." Storm sighed.

Before anyone could respond there was a knock on the door. "*Come in!*" Kendra shouted.

The door to the private room swung open and it was the wedding planner, Anita. "Ladies it's time for the lineup."

"Okay." Kendra then focused her attention back to Storm. "It's showtime, babes. Don't be a runaway bride now because we'll be waiting on you."

"I'll be back for you so sit tight," Anita informed Storm before closing the door.

Storm gulped hard and remained silent as her best friends walked out the door. The foursome had been cut down to three since one member of the group could no longer be trusted. She paced the floor for a good ten minutes before there was a knock on the door. Storm rubbed her hands together and blew into them.

"Okay, okay, it's time." The second knock was a little harder than the first one. *"Come in!"* she shouted.

"Wow! Look at my beautiful princess—all grown up now." Storm's father walked into the room wearing the most joyful smile and hugged her. "I'm so proud of the woman you've become, sweetheart."

"Thank you, Daddy."

Pulling his handkerchief from his breast pocket, he dabbed her eyes with it. "Is everything, okay?"

"Yes, I'm just nervous that's all." She sniffled.

There was no way she was about to mention the real reason she was shedding tears. If it wasn't for the waterproof, makeup her foundation would've smeared with all the crying.

"Don't be, everything is going to be okay. So, come on, it's time for me to give you away."

Storm grabbed her father's hand and they proceeded to leave the room. There was no doubt in her mind that she loved Dominic. For that reason, she was able to hold her head high and push those insecurities out of her head. It was her day and she was going to enjoy it to the fullest.

The sound of *'Let's Get Married,'* by *Jagged Edge* played softly throughout the church, as Storm walked down the aisle clutching her father's hand. Happiness took over her once she laid eyes on her handsome husband. Dominic was the true epitome of what a real man should be.

The wedding party was dressed to the nines and the decorations turned out better than expected. Dominic wasn't too pleased with the whole Rose Gold and Burgundy scheme, but he wanted to make his wife happy so he agreed. Storm took a quick glance at her bridesmaids, but something wasn't right. There was one too many, so she looked again. The sight of Jade's face made her want to drop her bouquet and lay hands on the trifling bitch that proclaimed to love her like a sister.

'What the fuck is she doing here?' Storm thought to herself.

Her first thought was to beat her ass on sight for disrespecting her, but she refused to ruin her special day. Instead of getting out of character she kept a smile on her face. Storm's father released the hold on his only child, passing her off to her husband. Dominic peeped her facial expression and immediately knew it was because of Jade's presence.

Being the charming man that he was, he kissed her hand and whispered in her ear. "Beautiful, this is your day, so don't let no one take that away from you."

Letting his words warm her spirit. She took a deep breath and prepared to step into her future. Dominic couldn't help but gaze into her eyes. That smile and the way her beautiful gown hugged every curve blew him away.

"You look good enough to eat," he mumbled watching her grin from ear to ear.

It felt so good to hold the woman of his dreams by the hand, waiting to say those magic words that would tie down that love forever. The ceremony was exquisite and every pew was filled up to the highest capacity. After the preacher spoke his encouraging words to the couple Storm recited her vowels.

"Dominic, from the first day we met, I knew that you were the one for me. You came into my life during my darkest moments and filled my days with nothing but sunshine. You are everything to me and life has no purpose without you. For the rest of my life, I promise to honor, cherish and treat you like the king you are. I'm forever yours until I leave this earth. I love you."

Now it was Dominic's turn. His heart pumped so fast and hard he could barely hear his own thoughts. It was the first time in his life he felt nervous about anything. A moment of silence filled the room as Storm soothed her hand across his shoulder for extra comfort.

"All my life I've always found myself chasing things that held no value. I tried to focus so hard on being the best man for my family and friends that I didn't know what I truly wanted for my own journey. Growing up I heard one statement from my father that stuck with me to this day. He told me out of all the choices you make you're gonna suffer from a lot of mistakes. And out of all those mistakes, you'll learn what not to do." Dominic paused briefly.

"That's what'll help you grow to be great. When I look at you I glow on the inside. I tried my best to repel against his words so much that it still proved to be a relevant fact. Even after all those bad decisions, I still ended up with the most beautiful woman in the world. I know, I can't speak for everyone on this planet, but that's more than great for a man like me. I've exceeded the limits of that meaning and I know for sure there's no word that can define the love I possess in my heart for you as my queen." Catching the tears that streamed down her face with his finger he finished. "If I had to go through every mistake, I made in my life again to make it back right here, I would smile every step of the way to reach the greatness that waits for me at the end."

Storm couldn't help but lean in and kiss her man's lips passionately.

"I think that's supposed to wait until after you two say I do," the pastor whispered under his breath." Realizing their love flow was at its peak, he placed the microphone to his lips. "Well, I guess I pronounce this eager couple husband and wife."

The church immediately broke out into a fit of laughter along with a loud applause. Dominic couldn't help but taste the sweet mint flavor that lingered on Storm's tongue as he held on to her waist.

"You better stop kissing me like that. It's nothing that can stop me from attacking you now, sir."

"The only thing that's gonna keep me from attacking you tonight is a steel wall," he replied seductively.

"If everyone can please follow me to the auditorium of the church, we can proceed with the wedding," Anita announced waving her arms for the crowd to make their way out.

The guests wasted no time clearing the building as she guided the attendants to their destination. Dominic did a double take after viewing the grand set up. The food that was specially catered smelled delicious. The unique champagne flute waterfall was definitely an eye-catcher. The burgundy designs matched everything accordingly and the six-layer wedding cake sat in the center of the room surrounded by white rose petals.

"It's beautiful," Storm said with excitement while glancing around the open room.

"I'm glad you love it. Anita did her thing in such a little time. Anything that makes you happy, I'm down with it," he agreed placing a kiss on her cheek. He felt a firm pat on his back and turned around to face Storm's father.

"Son, I just wanted to come tell you personally that this is a wonderful job you pulled on my baby girl's special day. This is a once in a lifetime thing and you made sure it was memorable."

"Thank you so much, sir. Your daughter is my heart and I wouldn't allow this day to turn out any other way," Dominic replied while shaking his hand.

As *112*'s hit single '*Cupid*,' began to pour from the DJ's speakers. Her father's facial expression brightened. "I don't wanna hold you kids up. Enjoy your day!"

"Thank you, Daddy." Storm laughed as he ventured off to mingle with the family.

Looking deeply into her eyes Dominic politely grabbed her wrist. "Do you mind if your husband has this dance?"

She grinned at his charming manners and placed her head on the center of his chest. Then he locked onto her hips and began to step with rhythm to the music that played smoothly in the air. Storm's joyous aura instantly crashed to the floor after spotting Jade camouflaged with the crowd directly across from them.

"Roguish ass bitch," she mouthed while mugging evilly.

"Baby, I expect better from you. Soften your anger and speak to her like a real woman," Dominic said catching her off guard. His eyes were closed, but he still moved along with the tunes as if all was normal.

"How in the hell did he just hear that?" Storm pondered silently with animosity written on her face.

"Your entire vibe just completely switched. I can feel the tension rising from your skin. In this world, you have two types of people. You have the weak minded and the respected. You're my queen which makes you a boss. Make her respect you!"

Kissing her forehead, Dominic nodded towards Jade and made his way over to the guests. Shaking harder than a two-dollar stripper on crack, Storm watched as Jade baby stepped her scary ass across the floor.

"Hey, Storm, you look so beautiful."

"Who in the fuck invited you to this event? I could've sworn I made myself perfectly clear on where we stood."

"Please just hear me out." Jade motioned her hand as if she was about to cry. "I know that I don't deserve to be in your presence, right now, because I did something that I can never take back. I can't remove your pain, neither can I reverse time to stop myself from making that stupid decision. All I can do is sincerely apologize and beg you to forgive me, Storm." She sighed. "You're like my sister. I don't want our friendship to end this way," she pleaded.

"You have the audacity to ask for forgiveness after you pulled that treacherous ass stunt? Jade, we were friends for years, I would've never betrayed you for any reason. I trusted your slutty ass and you stabbed me in the back. Look at my glamorous wedding and my handsome husband. You did all that shit to hurt me and I still won, Sweetie. For the last time please get it through your thick skull, I don't want to rekindle anything with you. We are not homegirls and you're not my fucking sister."

"Is everything okay over here?" Kendra intruded on the conversation with Tia on her heels.

"Everything's perfect," Storm replied with a fake smile. "Kendra, can you please do me a favor and escort this trash to the front door? I have a wedding to finish." Excusing herself from the circle, Storm joined Dominic.

"How did it go?" He asked in a genuine tone.

"She respected my choice, I don't want to think about it anymore."

Smooching her lips, he accepted the statement hoping that chapter for her was finally closed.

Chapter 9

Dominic and Storm walked along the shore of Montego Bay holding hands, as she sipped on a Rum Punch. The sun beamed down on them as the gentle breeze swayed the palm trees. She wiggled her toes in the warm, soft, white sand.

"It's so beautiful out here and the water is so blue."

"Not as beautiful as you."

"I get that from my mama." She giggled.

Dominic stopped and turned his wife facing him. The black, satin bikini and long sheer skirt made it hard for him to keep his hands off her. He roamed her body like he'd discovered new land, then stopped when he reached her backside. He kissed on her neck, Storm took a deep breath because she was anxious for them to make love.

"They need to hurry up and get our room together. I'm ready to make love to you, right now. My shit so hard I can break a piece of wood with it."

"I'm ready, too, this drink has me feeling lovely." Storm placed her hand on his chest and made a slow trail with her finger pass his navel. Just like Dominic, she found new land when she felt that he was stiff as a board.

"Oh, you, ready—ready." She laughed.

"Hell, yeah." He moved one hand and looked at his watch. "The room should be ready come on."

Dominic was eager to lay the pipe when they made it to the room, but their first sexual encounter had to be special. It was a long time coming, but her worth made the wait easy to bear. Storm was just as anxious. When she made it into the room, she placed her hand over her chest and gasped.

"Oh, my God, this is perfect." The lights were dim, which added romantic darkness. Several candles were lit sending out a pleasant aroma and the kingsize bed was covered with rose petals in the shape of a heart.

"Follow the trail of the rose petals." Dominic pointed towards the floor.

Storm sipped on her drink and followed his instructions, which ultimately led her into the immense bathroom. The Jacuzzi tub was filled with bubbles and more rose petals.

"His ass getting the deluxe package for this." She grinned. Quickly gulping the rest of her drink, she sat it down on the sink and removed her swim attire. After getting completely naked she stepped into the semi-hot water and sat down slowly.

"Oh, this feels good."

"I'm glad you like it." Dominic walked in wearing only the chocolate on his body while carrying two wine glasses and a bottle of champagne.

"Like it?" she huffed. "I love it and I love you, too." Seductively she eyed his package and licked her lips. He was definitely well endowed and it wouldn't be long before she would have everything he had to offer.

"I see who got your attention." He chuckled and poured champagne into both of their glasses. "Here."

Storm took the glass and tossed the whole thing back. "Give me another one."

"Damn, baby don't get too drunk. I want you to be alert for all of this." He stepped into the water and sat down. "This water hot. Did you pee in it?" He laughed.

"You so nasty." She giggled. "No, I didn't, that's nasty."

Dominic grabbed both of her feet, position them on his thighs and massaged them slowly. Storm leaned her head back and closed her eyes. "That feels good."

That only lasted so long before Storm sat up and made her way to his side. She straddled his lap, wrapped her arms around his neck and kissed him deeply. The chemistry between them was so intense he couldn't resist going further. Dominic slipped his hand into the water and stroked his dick. It didn't take much for his soldier to stand at attention. Swiftly, he parted her love petals and pushed past the tight barrier.

"Ssss—aaahhh!" Storm moaned loudly while squeezing him for dear life. She clenched her eyes tight and bit down on her lip preparing for the pleasurable pain she was about to face. Dominic gripped her waist, pushing her down further onto him. "Shit." She tried relaxing, but the width of his dick was stretching her apart.

Storm's arms were wrapped tightly around his neck. "Baby, loosen up before you choke me to death."

Instead of replying to him, she loosened her grip and allowed him to take control. Slowly, he thrust in and out of her super wet nookie with ease, while guiding her movements.

"Yeah, just like that," he whispered.

There was no doubt in his mind that she was indeed celibate. Her pussy was so tight it was like hitting a virgin all over again. Storm's walls were like the Great Wall of China. The sweet sounds of her moaning were music to his ears. Water splashed onto the floor, as Dominic became more aggressive.

After a while Storm leaned up and held onto the side of the tub and matched his rhythm. Now taking control, she rolled her hips in a circular motion.

"Yeah, fuck me back," he grunted.

"Mmmm—hhhmmm!" Storm bounced up and down at a steady pace, while he sucked and licked on her nipples.

Sex in the tub was cool and all, but Dominic was ready to go full throttle. The space was limited, and he couldn't put it down the way he wanted to. What she just received was a mere sample of what he could do. In the bedroom was where he prepared to give her the entrée and dessert. So, they went to their next location dripping wet walking across the cold floor.

"Lay down," Dominic instructed while standing next to the bed with his dick in his hands.

"You first." She insisted.

There was no need to debate because they had seventy-two hours to do every position known to man. Hell, they even had time to create some new shit. Dominic laid back on the bed, giving her complete control. Storm eased up on the bed next to him and positioned herself in the doggy style position. Making sure she gave him a full shot of what it looked like from the back. Gently, she stroked his dick and eased it into her mouth inch by inch.

It had been even longer since she'd given head. So, she schooled herself with a few Pornhub and XNXX videos for the special occasion. Gotti wasn't getting that because trust was an issue. She refused to put her mouth on an unfaithful dick. There was a lot of truth in the saying, the best dick is always dangling between the legs of a no-good ass nigga.

That was a thing of the past, so she pushed those thoughts out of her head and went to work on the man before her eyes. Storm's hand moved up and down, while she sucked and slurped on his piece. The constant wiggling of Dominic's toes confirmed she was doing her job. To add a little more excitement she massaged his balls at the same time.

"Shit." Dominic finally opened his mouth, while enjoying the view of her ass jiggling and pussy glistening with juices. Extending his arm, he played with her clit and smeared the juices on the crack of her ass. With ease, he inserted his thumb into her ass.

Storm hummed, but she couldn't speak with her mouth full. Feeling the sensation rise in his member, he quickly pulled back from her succulent lips. "You trying to kill me?"

"Let me find out you can't handle this!" She snickered.

"I see you got jokes." He stood to his feet heading for the kitchen area.

"Uh, where do you think you're going?" Storm questioned while eyeing his naked backside.

"Patience baby, I got that booty for seventy-two hours."

Giggling from his remark, she laid back anticipating his next touch. Her body was on fire as she closed her eyes placing a finger on her clit. The sexual tension was at its peak and continued to rise with every minute that passed. Feeling his presence, she looked up into his face as he towered over her. Dominic's hands carried a small can of ice and a plastic container of strawberries.

"You're cheating on me," he grinned seductively.

"I was just keeping it warm for you."

Bending down in between her legs, he pulled her closer to his face then placed a strawberry inside her plump pussy lips. He grabbed the open bottle of champagne and begin to pour the expensive drink down her thighs.

As he swirled his tongue in a circle Storm shivered. "Oh, my G— God," she stuttered.

Eating the fruit from her kitty, he cuffed his hands under her ass and raised it up. He held her body in the air and began to feast on her womanhood ferociously.

"Dominic," she panted while clutching the bed sheets. "Wait!"

Feeling a shortening of breath from his explosive escapade, her eyes rolled in ecstasy. Dominic's tongue was reaching delicate spots that begged to be scratched and her body felt as if it would melt through his fingers at any second. Determined not to waste any time, he flipped her over on all fours, grabbed a cube of ice and placed it into his mouth. He began to slowly kiss down the arch of her back. Storm bent over further while rolling her eyes in satisfaction. Dominic reached for her ass and spread both cheeks while putting his cold tongue directly in the center.

Storm's eyes glistened in euphoria as she uttered the words, "I love you!"

"Forever and ever, my queen," he replied while continuing his rampage.

After a few minutes of exploring her goodies, he raised up with his rod dripping heavily. The view of her slippery slit made him anxious, so he eased smoothly inside. Putting his hands on her juicy ass, he slid deeper causing her pussy to fart in delight.

"Babyyy," she whined feeling his length murder her walls.

As her orgasm erupted she moaned loudly with her face buried into the pillow. Dominic bit his bottom lip as he began to thrust harder. Storm's ass collided with his pole causing her to slightly jump.

"Where you going, huh?" He grunted locking onto her hips.

Storm's mind was in a trance. Her stomach felt as if it was balling into a knot as she held her breath from the punishment she was receiving. Watching her sweet spot coat his dick like glue, he backed out catching his breath. Rolling over to face him, she held her pussy with a sad expression.

"I think you proved your point, daddy."

"Let me find out." He teased while climbing on top of her and admiring the monster pumping between her thighs.

Storm pinched her nipples while kissing his lips. Dominic rubbed his hand through her smooth silky hair. Right after the wedding, she took down her bun, so she could wear her natural hair. While staring into her eyes he became hypnotized. That feeling alone let him know he was the luckiest man alive. From her love to her body, all the way down to her touch, it all felt so perfect.

"I love you," he whispered, feeling his climax rising.

"I love you, too," she moaned, rubbing the side of his face as a tear streamed down her cheek.

He released himself inside of her and planted soft kisses down her neck as he stroked softly back and forth. After the final drip, he rolled over and wrapped her in his arms. The moment felt so surreal, Dominic couldn't believe he was actually a happily married man.

"Are you, okay?" She asked with a light peck on his chest.

"As long as you're near me I'm always good beautiful." Dominic seized the moment and squeezed his wife tightly in his strong arms, so they could cuddle. Time passed quickly and they drifted off into a deep sleep.

***

Storm stirred out of her sleep and opened her eyes to a ray of sunlight casting down on her face. The sound of the ocean waves slightly crashing against the shore could be heard from the balcony and the aroma of breakfast flowed gently with the warm wind. Adjusting her naked body under the covers, she sat up to Dominic holding a silver platter of food.

"Good morning." He smiled.

She roamed her eyes down his bare chest, landing on his boxer print bulging directly toward her. His energy said he was ready to attack at any moment and the slight tingle between her legs gave a quick reminder of the breathtaking episode from last night.

"I think your little friend needs counseling, he's angry." She teased pulling the covers up to her nose.

"He don't mean no harm, baby. Are you hungry?" he replied sitting down next to her.

As he removed the silver tops on both plates, she stared at the scrumptious omelets and turkey bacon with a side order of fresh grapes and orange juice.

"I could go for something to eat. I think you knocked all of the food out of my stomach."

Laughing at her silly remark, he placed a wet kiss on her lips. "I wanted to go out and have a little fun today. I want you to eat and take a shower, so we can head out and see what the bay has to offer us. I won't rest until I know I've given you the best honeymoon ever."

"Aww, baby, you've already made me a happy woman by placing this ring on my finger."

"That's my job and it truly matters to me," he said while holding up her chin to look him in the eyes.

Storm watched him head toward the bathroom. Seconds later the sound of the shower water running caught her ears. She bit a small piece of omelet, following a few grapes and tossed back her orange juice. Then slid the comforter off her naked body and quickly followed Dominic's trail. The sound of the glass door sliding caught his attention. When he turned to face Storm, she was staring at him seductively, while sliding her tongue across her top lip. She stepped under the steamy water with him and stroked his manhood before kissing his solid chest. The drunk affection she placed on him kept his heart beating harder than a bass drum.

"You're supposed to be eating," he mumbled as she twirled his shaft back and forth.

"I'm about to eat, right now," she replied sliding down to her knees.

After thirty minutes of moaning and scratching, Dominic led Storm to the bed allowing her to lay down. He took the baby oil in his hand, then began to massage every part of her body. It felt so wonderful to pamper his woman and watch their relationship blossom into divine love. A deep love that would never end.

***

Hours passed and nightfall was now slowly approaching. Their entire day was filled with excitement from the five-star restaurant, down to the expensive shopping spree at every high-end designer store they passed. Finally getting back to their resort, they headed down to the beach. Kicking their shoes off Dominic held Storm as they sat in the sand viewing the sunset below the horizon. As she watched the water brush against their feet. She looked at him dazing out into the ocean as if he were dreaming.

"Where do you see us in five years baby?"

Pondering on his question she used her imagination to envision their future. "I see us far away from the states retired with a large home. I see us running a few businesses to keep our income flowing in. Traveling the world of course and taking our children to some of the most exciting places they can think of. Just living and loving life."

Dominic lowered his head, soaking in her words before looking back out at the moving waves.

"What's wrong, why do you look so sad?" She asked rubbing through his smooth hair.

"I just wanna be able to give you everything," he responded in a hurt tone.

"Dominic, I love you, and I know for a fact that you can give me whatever you want. That's something you have proven to me numerous times."

"But what if I can't?"

The question puzzled her mind because confidence was something she always spotted in Dominic since she'd first laid eyes on him. The normal nigga couldn't match his loyalty and damn sure not his bank account. He was more of the superhero who snatched her up from the pits of the evil world. There was no limit to how far he would go to please her so *can't* wasn't a word she was used to hearing out of his mouth.

Storm hugged his neck and laid her head against his shoulder. "Regardless of what you do for me, I'm just happy to be your queen, Dominic. That's the only thing that matters to me. I didn't marry you for what you can do. I did it because of your kind and genuine heart, baby. You're the perfect man for me, I wouldn't trade you for the world. You are my life, baby."

Nodding in silence, he held her close thinking of what awaited for their future.

Chapter 10

One week had passed since the couple returned from their honeymoon. Things were back to normal and work consumed them as usual. So, when Saturday rolled around Storm was happy to be off and catch up with her girls while Dominic handled some important business.

As she pulled into the parking lot she spotted Kendra's car and parked next to it. Tia spotted her and jumped out of the car, rushing in her direction with her arms out. Kendra was right behind her.

"Look at my friend. Girl, I thought you would be in a wheelchair when I saw you." They hugged and laughed.

"Really girl—a wheelchair." Storm giggled.

"Hell, yeah, I know that man broke your pelvis." Tia teased.

"Well." Storm tossed her head to the side, flicking her hair. "I'm not going to go into great detail, but he did break me off proper. Had my ass walking funny all weekend. You know it's good when he makes you shed a tear while he in it."

Kendra laughed and hugged her best friend. "Yeah, he don't realize that he just activated stalker behavior."

"I'm not worried about him doing nothing he ain't supposed to be doing. Besides he's not crazy. He knows I will fuck him up and whatever Dizzy Dora is brave enough to try me. I'm sweet, but y'all know I'll go there."

"Girl, he ain't shit like, Gotti. Dominic, is a real man and he knows he has a real woman on his team," Tia added.

"Okay, can we talk on the inside while we get this spa treatment because the sun is beaming down on us in case y'all don't feel it." Kendra turned on her heels to lead the way.

All three women were draped in white robes, with towels wrapped around their heads as they sat in massage chairs letting their feet soak.

"This was a must needed spa day." Storm exhaled. "My feet are killing me."

"Why, did he fuck the polish off your toes?" Tia giggled.

"Only you would say something like that." Kendra chuckled.

"So, that wasn't funny?" Tia was always the one cracking jokes.

"Hell, yeah, I never said it wasn't. I'm just saying it takes a special kind of fool to say some shit like that."

"You know something wrong with me."

"You got that right," Storm added.

Kendra turned in her seat to face Storm. "So, how does it feel to be married and when are you quitting your job?"

The conversation was a familiar one and certainly one she gave little thought. "Oh, my God, you sound like, Dominic. He wants me to quit my job and be a housewife, but I don't want to. I actually love my job and I love being independent."

"Girl bye." Tia couldn't wait to put in her two cents. "First of all, you should've stayed a single lady if you wanted to be so damn independent. You know damn well he ain't going for that. I guarantee within the next two months you'll be putting in your two-week notice."

"I'm going to miss you at work, but I think you should honor his wishes. He's the head of the household now and he's loaded your bank account with money, so you have no worries."

Storm thought about what her girls were saying for a minute before she replied, "I get what y'all saying, but I don't want to be a dependent. You see where that shit got Jade's dumb ass."

Kendra held her hand up to stop her from talking. "First of all, you and Jade, are nothing alike. She's stuck in her teenage years and you're on some grown woman shit. It's not like this is your boyfriend. This is your husband we're talking about."

She hit the nail on the head because those were straight facts. "Okay, I'm going to think about it. Especially since I'm ready to start a family with him."

"So, y'all ready to start pushing out babies already?" Tia stopped scrolling through her phone and looked up. "Girl, you better enjoy your husband for the first year because when those babies start popping out there will be no such thing as privacy."

"Well, Dominic, never mentioned having kids. That was all me."

"Shit, maybe he don't want any, right now."

"Well, he might as well because we've been having lots of raw sex since we tied the knot. Not once has he put on a condom, pulled out or ask me to get on birth control. Dominic knows what he's doing."

Storm's cellphone vibrated. When she looked at it, it was a text from Dominic.

Love of my Life//: Are you cooking dinner tonight?

My world//: Yes. What would you like?

Love of my Life//: Anything, as long as I can have you for dessert.

My World//: I guess we're having each other for dessert because that's what I had in mind. I've been fantasizing about sucking the skin off all day! ☺

Love of my Life//: You just made my dick hard. I'll see you at seven o'clock.

My World//: I love you, baby!

Love of my Life//: I love you, too! Have on something sexy for me.

My World//: Your wish is my command.

Love of my Life//: Damn, I love you!

My World//: Ditto, baby!

Storm was grinning hard when she put her phone away. When she looked up Kendra and Tia were staring at her.

"We don't have to ask who that was," Kendra smirked.

"Nope and I'm about to leave y'all."

"Why?" Tia whined.

Storm licked her lips and stuck out her tongue. "I have a big chocolate dick that I'm about to suck and fuck. We're still newlyweds and its baby making season."

71

Storm spotted the woman doing her pedicure and waved her hand in the air. "I'm ready for my polish, I have to go."

Thirty minutes later Storm was walking out of the door. The sun was still shining bright, but it wasn't too hot. She had two and a half hours to get things ready at home, including stopping by the store. Needless to say, she was on borrowed time. Nasty thoughts of Dominic crossed her mind, as she had a flashback of the amazing sex they have daily. She could feel her kitty throbbing and purring through her panties. Storm was definitely hooked on his pipe.

"I'm not the only one missing him." She giggled looking down at her phone.

Storm was so focused on googling a sex store that she had a bodily collision with someone walking down the sidewalk. Immediately, she rose her head to see who she'd hit.

"I'm so sorry, I didn't see—" Storm froze, and her mouth hit the concrete when she saw his face.

"Long time, no see. How you doing, baby?" Gotti asked with his arms folded.

The Mitchell & Ness snapback he wore hung low showing nothing but his dark cold eyes. His negative energy proved that he was far from excited and the Glock .40 handgun that rested on the left side of his hip was a solid clarification.

Taking a small step back, Storm's hands began to fidget out of fear. "G—Gotti, when did you get out?" she stuttered.

"Three days ago. Why? It ain't like you give a fuck," he spat glancing down at her finger. He grabbed her hand forcefully and stared at the large diamond ring with a lunatic expression. "What the fuck is this?"

"I thought I wrote you a letter explaining this already."

"And I could've sworn I wrote back telling you that shit was dead. I leave for a year or so and you just bounce to another nigga's dick like I had a life sentence or some shit."

Trying her best not to show any weakness, she muscled up the courage to speak her mind. "You have some big ass nuts talking to me like I'm some kind of fucking slut. You couldn't keep your dick to yourself. Then you have the nerve to slay that trifling bitch, Jade, and come home as if nothing happened. I've never stepped out or gave another man the time of day when I was with you. I'm the one who should be mad. You broke my heart and I'm finally surpassing that so I can be happy, Gotti. You did this to yourself," she said trying to move past him.

He blocked her path again, then took a step closer. "What about my side of the fucking story. You listen to this freak ass bitch instead of asking yo' man what happened? Sounds like you wanted to jump ship from the start."

"I've never had any reason to be unfaithful or leave you until now. I gave you my all and still received the shitty end of the stick. Just be a man for once and admit it."

"Admit what? That I'm human and make mistakes. I'm not perfect, girl. Never have been, but I bet everybody knows that I kept you first on my priority list. The same one who would lay that pistol game down to make sure I could take care of home. I guess none of that shit counts, huh?" he asked squinting his eyes.

"It only counts when your intentions are pure, Gotti. You did those things so I wouldn't be able to see the true you. I've never made you do anything and I've always made my own way since you met me. Maybe now would be the time to fix those priorities so the next woman won't experience the same dirty ass results."

As he squeezed the bridge of his nose, a large vein protruded from the side of his neck. Storm knew his anger could top the charts in a matter of seconds, and it could easily place her life in danger.

"You must don't get it, you belong to me! I can guarantee, you don't wanna play stupid and get hurt, all cause you in your feelings. Storm, if you make me do this I'ma kill you. Just say you ain't gonna be with me again and I'll kill you, right here, right now!"

Feeling her heart drop Storm's knees began to tremble knowing that he would make good on his words.

"Hey! Is there a problem over here?" A husky white security guard asked spotting the troubled expression on her face.

"Gotti, no," Storm mumbled, watching him reach for the handle of his gun.

"Do it look like it's a fucking problem? I'm just talking to my wife," he lied flashing a wicked smile.

"Well, this isn't the place for a family dispute. Take it elsewhere and keep it moving."

"Maybe you need to mind your damn business before I be the last person you ever speak to again," he threatened before turning his attention back to Storm.

"Please," she begged seeing the disaster that was about to occur.

He gripped her jaws with his right hand and placed a strong kiss on her lips. "You better pray that I don't find you. I'm gonna skin you and your little mystery man like a fucking fish. I promise!" Gotti spat with venom dripping from his statement.

He walked off, headed back to his rented vehicle and quickly got inside. After slamming his hand against the dashboard numerous times, he started the engine and pulled off.

***

As he sat at his kitchen table, Clyde quickly raised his head after hearing the doorbell ring. He strolled inside the living room. Then he glanced out of the front window and smiled to himself.

"It's about time, nigga. What the fuck took you so long?" He embraced Gotti after letting him in.

"You know how shit be the first few days a nigga touchdown. I'm collecting all that's owed to me and adding a few names to my death list."

"All you need to be worried about is adding some bankrolls to your pocket. We ain't petty hustling no more lil' cuz," Clyde bragged as he moved back towards the kitchen. "And as you can see we damn sho' ain't gotta take nothing."

Staring at the four kilos of cocaine, he picked up one from the table examining the product thoroughly. "How much of it is mines?" He asked with a serious look.

Knowing his cousin well, Clyde grabbed another brick tossing it to him. "Listen, Gotti, I'm only doing this because we family man. I can't take no slip-ups because my plug ain't shit to play with. All this nigga money gotta be on point. I need seventeen on both of those keys."

"Lame ass nigga you acting like I ain't never did this shit before. Calm down, I'll have that in two days, three at the most. Wassup with all this middle man shit anyway? I thought you was gonna link me up with this nigga so I can really get some paper?"

"Patience." Clyde laughed grabbing his shoulder. "Run ya' check up for a few days and I'll set it up for you. Trust me, you already in the door lil' nigga."

"Bet! After I lock that in I'm taking this bitch over piece by piece. If a muthafucka ain't working for us, they gonna either retire or get stamped on the back of a milk carton, simple."

Gotti ensured thinking about how he was going to make Storm regret ever crossing him out. It was hard enough dealing with the fuckery in the streets but losing her was something he couldn't tolerate. Nothing else held value like she did and the thought of another nigga sliding in between her legs made his flesh crave to kill a nigga.

"As long as we getting paper I wouldn't give a fuck," Clyde agreed rubbing his hands together.

"That's all I need to hear."

Chapter 11

Storm stood in the kitchen singing '*Trust and Believe*,' by *Keyshia Cole*, at the top of her lungs, while drowning her troubles with a bottle of wine. The dinner she promised Dominic was done and she was dressed in a black, lace gown. She couldn't wait for him to get home and take her mind off of things.

"You look so foolish, with my best friend. And she ain't no better than you, she's a three, I'm a ten. So, why are you calling my phone? You ain't got nothing I want. Thought we were really in love, but that was all a front."

The run-in with Gotti had her emotions and nerves severely scattered. He was the last person she expected to see. Especially since the online prison system didn't display a release date when she looked him up. She placed the glass on the counter and took a deep breath.

"How the fuck did he get out?"

Storm pondered over every possibility of his early release but came up with nothing. Snitch wasn't in his vocabulary, so that option was out of the question. As bad as she wanted to hate him she couldn't. Her mind and heart were torn between the two. It was like battling the angel and devil on both shoulders. She just wished the duo would get on one accord and dismiss him forever.

Deep down she still loved him, but forgiving him for committing the ultimate betrayal was out of the question. Out of all the hoes in Atlanta, he chose her best friend. Gotti needed to save his gangsta tactics for his enemies and accept the fact that their relationship was over. In Gotti's case that would be too much like right. One well-known fact about him was that he never issued out a threat and not followed through with it. Storm's phone lit up, as a text message came through. Looking down at the screen she realized it was an image from Tia, but before she could open it, she was calling.

"Hello."

"Girl turn that music down, sheesh."

Storm picked up the remote from the counter and lowered the volume. "What's up?" she slurred.

"Are you drunk?"

"I'm trying to get there." Storm took another sip of wine and sat it back down on the counter. "What's up?"

"Girl, did you see that fine ass man I sent you."

"What fine man?"

"Open it and look. Girl that man done got finer than a bitch."

Storm opened the messaged and before her eyes was a picture of Gotti, posing with one of his homeboys at the gas station with no shirt on. She couldn't deny that his body wasn't appealing, but his threat wouldn't leave her mind.

"Child, I guess."

"Wait. You saw him, didn't you? That's why you playing that song in the background."

"I don't know what you talking about." She lied.

"You wanna fuck him don't you?"

Silence took over the conversation, causing Tia to laugh at her refusal to answer. "Storm do not mess up your marriage for no goddamn, Gotti. He don't deserve shit, but your ass to kiss. Did you forget everything he put you through?"

"Tia stop!" Storm used her hands to cover her face. The effects of the wine had kicked into high gear. "It's not what you think. I saw him, but it wasn't pleasant. He's mad because he saw the ring. Oh yeah, he said he's going to kill me and Dominic."

"See now he want to get out and play these crackhead ass games. Did you tell, Dominic?"

"No."

"Are you going too?"

"No, he's just mad, right now. Besides he doesn't even know, Dominic. Just stop worrying everything is going to be okay."

"Don't have that man walking around town not knowing that someone wants to kill him. That ain't right."

Staring at the clock, she realized Dominic was due home in ten minutes and she needed to be prepared for his arrival. Sulking about another man wasn't a good look and would definitely cause problems in her marriage.

"I have to go, Dominic will be home in ten minutes and I need to be ready for him. Talk to you later."

"Tell him, bye."

Storm couldn't help but open the picture once more. Tia ain't never lied. Gotti was finer than ever and the gray sweatpants did no justice for the package he carried in his boxers. His body was covered in tattoos and his six-pack was on point.

"Damn." She laid her head down on the counter. "Why am I looking at you like this?"

The phone was still in her hand, as she salivated over her ex. Storm jumped when she felt a pair of hands on her hips. "You scared me."

"What you doing?" Dominic sat his briefcase on the floor.

Closing the phone, she sat it face down on the counter and turned to face him. "Texting Tia." She wrapped her arms around his neck and planted a kiss on his lips. "I've missed you so much."

"I missed you, too."

Explicit thoughts of Gotti was on her mind heavily and she had to get rid of them. Maybe Tia was right about her wanting to fuck Gotti. Storm became aggressive as she unbuttoned Dominic's pants.

"Baby." He chuckled. "What's gotten into you?"

"You, so come on. I want you to fuck me right here on the kitchen counter."

Storm removed her gown and threw it on the floor. Then hopped onto the counter, she opened her legs and placed her feet on both stools. Dominic was stripping out of his clothes.

"Baby hurry up," she purred while rubbing her clit.

He walked up and moved her hand. "I'll handle that."

Dominic put her fingers into his mouth and licked the juices from them. Then placed his mouth on her pussy and sucked on it like a Georgia peach. Storm's eyes rolled to the back of her head, as she gripped the counter.

"Shit," she panted and pushed his head further into her sweet spot.

Dominic stayed down there until her pussy squirted juice into his mouth and down his throat. He stood on his feet, wiped his mouth and licked his lips. Storm was too anxious, so she pulled him close to her and wrapped her legs around his waist.

"Fuck me."

"I don't know what's got into you, but I love it."

Bending his knees, he squatted low enough to slip into her juicy tunnel and go deep. He gripped her ass from the back, slid her close to the edge and held her in place so she couldn't move. The first few strokes were slow, but he quickly switched gears on her ass. Storm moaned and called his name while he fucked her crazy.

"Ooohh fuck me, baby." Storm kissed him sloppily on the lips and rocked her hips to stay on rhythm with his strokes. "Ah—ah—ah! Beat this pussy—beat this pussy, baby!"

"Who pussy this is?" he asked.

"Yours," she moaned.

"You love me?"

"Yes, Daddy, I love you and only you."

Storm loved Dominic without a doubt, but she needed to reiterate that to her brain and heart since they seemed a little confused. For the next thirty minutes, Dominic beat the brakes and gas line out of her pussy. Storm couldn't move, so she just laid across the counter out of breath.

Dominic smacked her on the ass and chuckled. "You alright? Cause that's what you asked for."

"Yes." She smiled. "Now you have to carry me to the bed. My legs are numb."

"I got'chu, baby."

He scooped her up and took her to their bedroom. Storm crawled underneath the covers and closed her eyes. Dominic fucked every thought about Gotti out of her head and she was able to drift off into a deep, yet peaceful sleep.

***

"Jade, I'm gonna tell you like I did the first time. I don't know if you're really listening. Leave it alone and the rest will work itself out. Now just isn't the time," Kendra spoke through the receiver.

"But Storm doesn't even consider me a friend anymore. She hates me. How can something better happen out of that? It's like I'm being pushed away.

Sighing deeply Kendra massaged her temples. "Look, right now, you will only make yourself look more pathetic, and guilty. Storm, is doing her and living life. You continuing to show up with all this regret will make it more awkward. It's not like anyone put a gun to your head and made you fuck, Gotti."

"But you said—"

"To shut up and give the girl some time. That's what I'm saying now. Hell, after a while she ain't gonna give a damn honey. Pull ya' panties out yo' grandma shaped ass and chill. I don't need you calling my phone every thirty minutes with another sob story. If you just sit back all will unfold in a timely fashion. She probably miss you too, girl. Have you thought about that?"

Hearing the doorbell ring, Jade wiped the small tear from her eye. "You're right I just got to get it together and wait until she's comfortable. I'll just call you tomorrow. Maybe we can go out for lunch."

"Yeahhh, that might not happen. I got jury duty and I might not leave the courthouse until sun break. I'll let you know."

"Okay, maybe we can try another day," Jade replied.

"Sure thing," Kendra huffed before hanging up.

The bell ringing again caused her to set the phone down and quickly moved toward the door. Without checking to see who it was on the other side. She opened it and fear instantly caressed her body. Numbness began to overtake her feet as Gotti blew the smoke from his potent blunt of weed into her face.

"Gotti, what are you doing here? I—I thought that you were in prison?" She shook her head while looking back and forth between him and his young shooter.

"Bitch, it's cold out here. You ain't gone show no manners and let us step inside." He mugged.

His negative energy was pumping like a heater on a sunny day and slamming the door to lock it didn't seem like the smart thing to try and pull at the moment. Rubbing her index finger nervously she stepped to the side allowing them to enter. Dumping the ashes on the clean floor, Gotti glanced around the house and noticed that she was alone.

"Got anything to drink?" he asked blinking his red bloodshot eyes.

"Uh, I think so." Jade stepped into the kitchen checking the refrigerator. She couldn't help but feel his dark menacing stare beaming at her from the small distance between them.

Pulling two wine coolers out of the box, she quickly handed them to both men as if she was on a time limit. Staring down at the glass bottle in his hand, Gotti smirked before chuckling to himself.

"Gotti, is there any particular reason you're here? I was just about to head out and meet the girls." She lied with shakiness tainting her tone.

Gotti slammed the wine cooler against the wall causing Jade to jump and take a large step back.

"I just wanted to ask you a question or two," he said calmly. "It's kind of strange that I come home to find so much shit out of order. Not only do I gotta take back my streets. I gotta take back my own bitch. Now with that being said, a freaky bird told me I could ask the lovely Jade what the fuck was going on?"

"I don't understand what you mean." She pouted like a lost child.

"Did you tell Storm about what happened between us?"

The question caused her stomach to rumble heavily. Staring into his wide eyes, she tried to think of any excuse that would help her out of the sticky situation.

Gotti slammed a hard, right hand across her face, causing her body to crash to the floor. "Bitch, you must can't hear?"

"If she didn't, she damn sho can now." The young hustler laughed while leaning against the wall.

"Shut the fuck up nigga," Gotti ordered before looking back at Jade.

Tears began to flow down her face as she held her jaw in pain.

"Now when I decided to break away from this petty situation you do something stupid. There was nothing in the agreement about telling Storm anything. You knew that would make her walk away

82

from me and you got the nerve to play dumb. How do you suppose we change that?"

"I didn't mean for that to go down, I swear. All this was just a big mistake. I never wanted Storm to leave you."

"Too bad, cause that's what happened. You made all these twists and turns and now you gotta fix it. Tell me how can I get my bitch back, huh? I need to hear this shit."

"I don't know," Jade answered truthfully feeling she would be slapped again for being right.

"Or maybe I should just blow yo' shit back," Gotti mumbled showing the handle of his gun. "You need to remember who the fuck I am and learn how to keep your damn mouth closed. I guess you were gonna tell her how it all played out, too? I got my eye on yo' dumb ass. One more slip up from you could be critical. Please be careful." He threatened pointing his finger inches away from her face. After she nodded in compliance, he turned around and smoothly walked out of her home.

Jumping behind the wheel, Gotti started the ignition and slowly pulled off.

"Yo' bro, what if that bitch calls them folks on us? You probably need to handle that."

"You sound dumb as fuck. If I kill that bitch everybody in the city will pin that shit to me. These bitches ain't gonna accept that hoe coming up dead. She got enough common sense to sit down somewhere before shit gets ugly. The next time I'ma hide her ass in a ten-foot ditch."

Feeling the phone vibrate inside of his pocket, he pulled it out and answered. "Nigga it damn sho ain't time for me to pay you. So, wassup?"

"Miss me with all that," Clyde replied, blowing off the slick remark. "I did what you asked and things actually played out perfect.

"With what?"

"You meeting my plug. He said we can set up something, so I need to know you're ready. I told you this ain't no part-time hustling, nigga."

"I'm always ready. I don't know what type of nigga he is. I truly don't give a fuck. I'm trying to take my city back. We just need a push."

"Well, you about to meet the right man that can make of all that possible. Make sure you're over here in the a.m."

Gotti hung up, smiling knowing shit was finally about to shift. Once he reclaimed the streets everything would belong to him— *everything.*

Chapter 12

Storm walked through the house beaming like she had just won the lottery. After last night's episode, she was prepared to start her day with a smile. No one or nothing could ruin her mood. Not even Gotti with his threats or the treacherous Jade. When she walked into the kitchen Dominic was standing there thumbing through his phone looking good enough to eat in a three-piece suit.

"Somebody's in a good mood." Dominic leaned over and planted a kiss on Storm's lips while slipping his phone into his front pocket.

"Hmm, I wonder who's responsible for making that happen." Storm turned on her heels and opened the fridge.

"The king, baby."

Taking a water bottle from the fridge, she took the top off and took a sip. "You got that right."

"I don't know what got into you last night, but hopefully, it will return."

Storm looked him up and down then bit her bottom lip. Heavy lust lingered in the air like weed smoke. "Oh, I can definitely make that happen again."

Dominic cleared his throat and picked up his briefcase. "Don't threaten me with a good time. I'm heading out. Are you coming or do you have to make coffee?"

"No, I'm going to Dunkin' Donuts to get me a Latte."

"Well, come on so we can walk out together."

Dominic locked up the house while Storm walked to her vehicle. Standing a foot away, all movement came to a halt. The sight before her made her blood boil before shouting. "What the fuck?"

The hostility in her voice caused Dominic to rush over. "Bae, what's wrong?"

"Two of my tires are flat." She pouted. "Now I'm going to be late for work dealing with this shit."

"I can take you to work, that's not a problem," he suggested.

"That's okay, babe. I'll wait on a tow truck to come because I don't want to be stranded at work."

"See if you would've quit your job like I told you, we wouldn't be having this conversation, right now." Dominic shook his head then handed her his keys. "Just take my truck, I'll get you some new tires."

"Are you sure, babe? I know you have important things to do, I don't want to get in the way of that." Storm's eyes drifted to the windshield. Plain as day was a note. Instantly her heart started to race, but she couldn't panic because Dominic would notice. "Umm, babe. Can you put my bag in the truck and start it for me please?"

He grabbed the bag from her hand. "You lucky I love spoiling you. On a serious note, you need to consider quitting your job. I don't want my wife working. I'm the head of the household, that's my job."

"Staying at home all day would be so boring. It's not like you will be here with me to keep me entertained." Storm pouted and folded her arms.

"In due time, I'll be quitting, too." Dominic winked at her and walked off.

Storm didn't hesitate to retrieve the note and shove it into her pocket. Her mind was moving a mile a minute. The only person responsible for the note was Gotti and that meant Jade was behind it all.

"This hoe is really trying to ruin my marriage," she mumbled, walking toward the truck.

Dominic was just ending a phone call. "They will be here in thirty minutes. You go ahead to work, I'll see you later."

"I love you!" Storm tip-toed and gave him a kiss.

"I love you, too!"

Storm waited until she'd made it to the stop sign up the street from the house before pulling out the note. Just as she suspected, it was from Gotti. She opened it and read it out loud.

Hey, my love. As you can see, I know where you live. So, there is no place you can go and not be found. Didn't I tell you that? I will scorch the earth before I let another nigga, have you. We will be together like you promised. I'll see you soon, I love you, baby!

Storm screamed and ripped the note to pieces. "Why can't you just leave me the fuck alone?"

It was probably a good idea to tell Dominic what was going on since he knew where they lived, but that wouldn't be good. That would only cause problems in her new marriage and that was a risk she wasn't willing to take. The sound of a horn blowing startled Storm. She looked behind her and put on her emergency signal.

"Go around shit." She fished around inside her purse for her phone. "I can't go to work like this."

After she called the attendance hotline, she finally pulled off and left the neighborhood. Storm was ready to cause a violent disturbance. The true meaning behind her name. Atlanta traffic was the absolute worst, especially when on a mission. Storm weaved in and out of traffic before slamming on brakes and missing the car in front of her by a smidgen.

"Slow down Storm before Dominic kills you for wrecking his damn truck." She took a few deep breaths to try and calm herself down, but that didn't help at all.

It took damn near an hour for Storm to reach her destination. Once she parked in the driveway she removed her name tag and wedding ring, then tossed it into the middle console. The neighborhood was quiet, but all of that was about to change in a matter of seconds. After getting out of the car, she walked on the porch and rang the doorbell. As she rocked on her heels, she swung her arms back and forth waiting anxiously. No one came to the door, so she pressed it again. Finally, she could hear the locks click, then the door opened. Jade stood there wrapped in a towel. It was obvious she was surprised by the impromptu visit.

"Storm." She sighed. A bit of relief came over her because all she wanted to do was apologize until she forgave her. "I thought you would never talk to me again. I'm happy to see you. Come in!"

Storm didn't say anything as she stepped inside the house. Jade closed the door and turned around to face her. "I was about to get dressed, but that can wait, come sit down. Do you want something to drink?"

She shook her head. "I won't be here long."

"What's going on? Kendra said to give you some time, but that came faster than I thought."

"I'm confused as to why you feel it was necessary or even smart to tell Gotti where the fuck I live. Bitch, haven't you caused enough chaos in my life?"

That wasn't the reply Jade was expecting. "Storm, I didn't tell, Gotti, anything! He's lying to you."

"You must think I'm stupid." Storm raised her hand and slapped her across the face. "Fuckin' him wasn't enough for you? You're trying to ruin my marriage, too?"

Jade placed her hand over her cheek. "I wouldn't do that, I've already caused you so much pain. Storm, I swear, I didn't tell him where you lived. You gotta believe me!"

"Hoe I don't trust you." Storm reflected back on what she said about Kendra. "And let me tell you something, Kendra, cannot make me talk to you. I never told her I would. So, don't let her get your hopes up."

"Then why are you here, to rub it in my face?" Jade screamed.

The outburst caused Storm to lash out and hit her in the face. "Bitch, who you yelling at?"

Jade clutched her towel and tried to back up to keep from getting hit again, but she stumbled and that's when Storm caught her with an uppercut. Jade's body dropped to the floor. Storm pounced on top of her and attacked furiously. Throwing left and right hooks to her face and body, Jade kicked and screamed, but she didn't fight back.

"I didn't do it—I didn't do it!" she repeated and balled up into the fetal position.

Storm realized there was only one fighter, so she stopped and took a few steps back. "I'm telling you, right now, stay the fuck away from me and I mean it! I let you slide at my wedding for the sake of my husband, but as you can see, he can't save you. Whatever you and Gotti's punk ass got going on, leave me out of it."

Storm was still pissed, but it was time for her to go, so she headed toward the door.

"Storm, I love you, and I'm sorry."

"Fuck you hoe, just die already and take that fake love with you." Storm didn't bother looking back, as she slammed the door behind her.

***

As he fired up the blunt, Clyde nodded his head to the loud music. The meeting was in fifteen minutes and it was definitely no room for being late. As he sat in the passenger seat, Gotti stared out of the window with a blank expression. As Clyde passed the weed, he reached over turning down the volume.

"Don't even think about turning that shit back up. I can't focus on business while a nigga screaming through the radio about dodging the fucking Feds."

"Nigga, you ain't been worried about the police. I thought you run the mean streets of Atlanta? You shoulda got some Dre beats if you wanted to ponder on how to ask a nigga for the bricks." Clyde laughed feeling the Kush kick in heavily.

"Fuck you, lame. You musta forgot, I robbed all your other connections and left their asses stanking. The only reason I stopped is because you kept crying about me fucking up that petty ass change you was making. I'm trying to do this the right way," Gotti replied in a serious tone.

Staring at him from the driver's seat, Clyde screwed up his face. "Look, cuz, I'm just talking shit man. I don't need you trying to lay this man down. I ain't got time to be beefing with my boss man. Everything is gonna be a'ight. There's no need to get on any fuckery.

"Scary ass nigga shut the fuck up. Ain't nobody finna rob this nigga unless his ass play stupid. I'm just not good with accepting a no. If he fucks with me, he gets my loyalty—simple."

After grabbing the joint, Clyde inhaled. "I can guarantee he will give you a chance, bro. All he wants is his money on time and to watch us get rich together. The man dumping nigga's asses off about that loot, straight up."

"Yeah, yeah, I heard you the first time. The nigga go, Superman about his lil' money. Who gives a fuck? All the money we making will be on point every time. Besides, once we come up we might be serving his ass."

Ten minutes later Clyde was making a left down Piedmont Road. Turning inside the large car lot, he pulled up to the front entrance and shut off the vehicle.

"What the fuck are we doing here?" Gotti questioned.

"Just chill and follow me. Kill all the hard ass shit, too. I ain't tryna scare these people at the front desk."

Letting the remark slide pass his ears, he got out of the car trailing his cousin until they reached the customer service counter.

"Can I help you, gentlemen?" Jacob asked before they could speak to his employee.

"My name is, Clyde. Tell the boss man I need to see him please."

Before he could reply Dominic stepped out of the office door waving them to the back. They proceeded until reaching the spacious meeting room.

"Please come in and shut the door."

"I appreciate you taking the time to meet with us. This is my cousin I was telling you about."

"The name is, Max." Gotti lied looking him in the eyes. He could tell from the tailored suit that he was for sure playing with some commas.

"You can just call me, Bossman or D. Your cousin tells me, you're quite the hustler we've been needing. I've been searching for new help that can come push this business up a notch."

"Yeah, I hustle. I do whatever necessary to get that paper. I'm a true street nigga, so chasing the check is a lifestyle for me. I'm just not into going out bad. Period," Gotti emphasized with his fingers shaped like a pistol.

"We've been running through the blocks and hoods letting our face be known. Max is my way of touching bases with some new connections and buyers throughout G.A." Clyde added trying to sweeten the sound of his cousin's rough words.

"That sounds great but all money isn't good money. I can have one customer that buys me out and I'll still eat the same way. There's no reason to keep exposing yourselves to anybody. My product has no face. It's the taste that counts. I do have personal things I must attend to, so I'll make this easy for you both. How much do you think you can handle?" Dominic asked staring at Gotti.

"How much I can handle is not the question. Tell me how much you need to be moved and it's done."

Whistling in the air, Dominic rubbed his chin. "What I need to be moved is impossible to get rid of in two or three weeks. I've learned well in the game to never push someone so much because you'll eventually push too hard. I've been to numerous of different states and countries meeting very important people. And for some reason, they're still using the same method as me."

"Well, I'm sorry to tell you this, Bossman. But I don't know anything about methods on getting out here to hustle. I was taught to beat my fucking feet until every last pack was gone. Living in the streets taught me one thing also. If you can snatch your status from the bottom and make it to the top. You can make it anywhere. The grind ain't in ya method. It's in your heart. Now if you ain't got heart," Gotti said interlacing his fingers. "You've already lost when you step foot into this profession."

Dominic couldn't help but respect his mind frame. The average hustler never knew what it took in order to survive in the sick twisted ways of the drug game. It was never about who had the most money, nor the fear you could place in someone. It was the heart that separated the predators from the prey. The respected from the weak minded. A true grinder from a pickup boy.

"I don't trust many people, but I have to say, I do respect that. It's hard to find a hand full of men that know the difference between a strong heart and a reputation. The status doesn't mean shit if nobody really has love for you. You would just be a hustler holding a spot until the next man has enough heart to take your position. I'll start you off with ten. Seventeen off every kilo is mine. If you can push them off in a decent amount of time, I'll double the second package," he offered with his hand out to seal the deal.

Reaching pass Clyde, Gotti agreed with a firm shake. "Deal."

"Good, I will contact Clyde and get that to you fellas by the end of the night. If all goes well, you can be a very rich man." Dominic said tossing him a set of keys.

"What's this?"

"Clyde said you just came home from prison. It shouldn't be any reason you're late to make it somewhere. It'll be sitting in the front for you. Like I said, it gotta be in the heart."

Gotti smiled and headed out of the room with Clyde just a few steps behind him.

"I told you my plug was the fucking man."

"Yeah, you right," he replied, clicking the alarm on the key ring as they stepped through the double doors.

Spotting the all-white 2017 Dodge Demon, he gripped the sleeve of Clyde's shirt. "I think I got a new fucking friend. Fuck that, my new plug," he mumbled with a devilish grin.

Chapter 13

"I'm so fuckin' pissed, right now," Storm shouted, hitting the steering wheel and fighting back the tears.

"What's wrong, boo?" Kendra asked, placing a hand on her shoulder.

"You won't believe this shit."

"Try me."

Storm sighed deeply. "So, I get up this morning so I can head to work, only to see that I had two flat tires and a note from Gotti on my damn windshield."

"You're right, I don't believe that."

"Hell, me either, I'm just so fucking sick of him. I don't understand why he won't leave me alone? Like, bruh, you fucked somebody who was supposed to be my sister. There's no coming back from that."

"Girl, that's a typical man. They can sling dick wherever they please and the minute you give another nigga conversation you a whole hoe out here. It's not fair, but that's life." Kendra leaned against the door. "At least you have a real man, now, so you don't have to worry about that anymore."

"I know and it's like he don't understand that he hurt me. The type of heartache he caused wouldn't allow me to take him back even if I was single."

"What do you mean he don't understand?" Kendra's brow creased.

"After I left y'all at the spa, I ran into him outside. He wasn't happy when he saw my ring."

"Oh, yeah, Tia told me about that," Kendra smirked deviously. "She showed me that picture of him, too. Prison did, Gotti's body good. You sure you don't want to sample that?"

Storm cut her eyes deep into Kendra's face. "Are you serious, right now? I'm telling you what's going on with me and you making jokes about me fucking him."

"I'm sorry, Storm! I'm just trying to cheer you up."

"Now, isn't the time, Ken. This is serious and he's threatening my marriage. If Dominic, gets wind of this I don't know what he'll do or how he'll react."

"Don't get upset, but maybe you should meet up with him and hear him out. Get his side of the story. All you know is that he fucked her. You don't know all the details of that night."

Storm shook her head. "That's not a good idea. Nothing good can come from me and Gotti meeting up. Dominic, would kill me if he ever found out."

"And how will he know, are you going to tell him? Cause I'm sure as hell ain't saying nothing."

Storm was silent, as she stared out the window in deep thought.

"Are you thinking about it?" she asked.

"No, I'm not doing that to my husband."

"Listen, apparently, Gotti has done his homework because he knows where you live. My best advice is to meet up with him and bury those old feelings before he does something you will regret."

Kendra paused for a second before she continued. "I mean unless the feelings are still there, and you're scared you might sleep with him."

Storm ignored the suggestion of her secret desire to sleep with Gotti. Especially after fantasizing about him while fucking Dominic in the kitchen. "He knows where I live because of, Jade. That bitch told him where to find me. All of this shit is her fault."

"You think she would do that?"

Storm became frustrated, all signs pointed to Jade. She was the only person with a connection to Gotti and that led her to believe she was hiding more than she admitted to. Her behavior was similar to a psychotic side bitch.

"Who else would tell him? Dominic, is low key. No one knows where we live. Not even his workers. It's like she's trying to ruin my marriage after ruining my relationship. That's why I beat her ass this morning."

"You right." Kendra nodded her head. "Maybe she feels bad and is trying to make things right between you and Gotti. I will admit that she seems really apologetic about what she did. I told her to give you some time and maybe you'll come around. Maybe even have a sit down with her, but I explained that it has to be on your terms."

Storm rolled her eyes and sucked her teeth. "Yeah, that's not happening. I wouldn't give a damn if, Jesus Christ, himself sat down on my sofa and told me I had to forgive her in order to get to heaven. I'm not doing it!"

"Really, Storm?" Kendra couldn't believe she was so adamant about not even considering forgiving Jade for the sake of not carrying on a grudge.

"Yes, I'd rather go to hell."

Kendra scratched the side of her head then held up one finger in the air. "Hold up. You said you beat her ass this morning? What happened—where?"

"After finding the note before, Dominic. I went to her house and confronted her about it. She tried to act like she didn't do it like I'm stupid or some shit."

"That's fucked up. She been jealous of you and our relationship since day one. I been peeped it, but I never said anything because I was new to the group. Then after a while, she became cool."

"Fuck that bitch, I hate her."

Kendra ignored her comment. "So, this is why you called out today?"

"Yeah, I wasn't in the mood."

Kendra took her phone out of her shirt pocket and hit the side button. "Are you coming in?"

"No, I'm about to go downtown to kill some time and blow off some steam before I go home. I can't be in a foul mood around, Dominic, because he'll see right through the bullshit."

"Okay, girl. I have to go because my break is up. I'll talk to you later."

"Okay."

Kendra leaned over and gave Storm a tight hug. "Everything is going to work out and before you know it things will be the way they are supposed to be."

After Kendra got out of the truck, Storm sat in the parking lot contemplating whether she should tell Dominic about what was going on. The last thing she needed was him to be blindsided by her past. Although he was very understanding of every situation she came across, this scenario was quite different. She knew Gotti was dangerous, but so was Dominic. The only difference was she never saw that side of him since they'd been together. He was well respected in the streets, so no static ever came their way.

Storm's mind drifted back to Gotti. Deep down a part of her still loved him, but she wasn't in love with him. "Maybe I need closure to move on," she mumbled.

She pulled out of the parking lot, drove in silence and she could hear the advice her father gave her a long time ago.

"If you don't heal from what hurt you, then you'll bleed on the one that didn't cut you."

It all made sense to her but meeting up or even having a conversation could ruin the best thing that ever happened to her in life and that was finding the perfect man. Gotti was the type of person to take what he wanted. So, fighting for her, or even a little gunplay was nothing when it came down to it. He'd made that very clear the other day.

***

It was starting to get late in the evening as Dominic pushed his whip through the Cobb county streets. The new operation that was being placed in effect was bouncing around in his head by the second. In order for shit to run smoothly, loose screws would have to be tightened.

"What time should I be expecting you home?" Storm asked. Her current problem was starting to become more exhausting and all she wanted at the time was to be held.

"I shouldn't be more than an hour love. Is everything okay?" he replied, hearing the sadness in her tone.

"I just want you next to me."

"Fifty-nine more minutes and I'll be kissing you gently on the lips. Promise!"

"I love you, Dominic."

"I love you more."

Ending the call, he drove down Franklin Road and parked in front of the two-story crib. After honking the horn twice, he glanced at his watch and eased back into the seat. Before his patience could run thin Juve stepped out of the house and slowly headed for the truck. He climbed inside and shut the door behind him exhaling deeply.

"Yo', what's good, D? Congratulations on the marriage man. I hate that I couldn't make—"

"Where's my money, Juve?" Dominic asked not trying to hear the small talk.

"I'm still trying to come in on that, Dominic. My pockets sitting on E and the motion ain't working in my favor."

"Thirty-five grand. I've been waiting patiently three months for thirty-five grand. I spared you on some time so I wouldn't have to hear any excuses. When I gave the package to you, I asked was it too big for your hands. You blew that question off as if it wasn't even possible. Is there something I'm missing? Or maybe you're too high to give me that answer also."

The malice in his voice only made things worse. No one truly had the courage to tell a big ass nigga like Dominic that his dope was being sampled and passed around like a fucking tea party. Excessive lying always caused stronger tension and Juve proved daily that he wasn't able to show gratitude by completing his obligation to the game.

"I fucked up, D, damn!" he yelled with both hands on his forehead. "I hustle and hustle over and over so I can survive. So, I can maintain my position out here. I just moved a little too fast and took a small loss."

"That's gotta be the weakest shit I've ever heard come out of a man's mouth. You hustle to win, not to fail, nigga. Taking losses comes from the hustler's hands, not the streets. Nobody woke you out of your sleep and ordered you to become a drug dealer. You owe me paper and you're starting to become a serious problem to everything

I got going on. I have a wife to take care of, so whatever you're speaking on is irrelevant if you're not pulling my bread out yo' pocket."

"I just need one more week, bro. I'll have it, that's my word. I'm gonna have it."

"Cool," Dominic replied smoothly.

Sometimes the best decisions were meant to be kept a secret. Saying the wrong thing could easily send a scary motherfucker over the edge. Even far enough for the police to get involved. As Juve departed from the car, Dominic dialed a number on his cell before pulling away from the curb.

"What's up, Bossman?" Clyde answered on the second ring.

"Put Max on the phone."

* * *

The thought of going out to put in some work had Gotti's blood boiling with anticipation. The extra fifty thousand Dominic offered was also a major plus. There were no limitations when it came down to chasing guape in his eyes. It was always business, never personal.

"I just need you to remember that we are in a hot ass junkie rental. Please try not to go overboard. Cobb county hanging a nigga like the early 1900s, and I ain't built for a two-hundred-year bid."

"That's because you ain't no street nigga. Do you wanna turn the car around, so I can drop you off at the house?" he asked Clyde with a mean expression.

"I'm just saying, cuz. I don't want the police waiting for us by the time I pull back up to my spot. I'm trying to move smart, not dumb."

In Gotti's head, it was officially time to lay down the rules. No one controlled his actions and nobody was getting in between him and the extra payday that was much needed.

"Pull over."

"*Pull over*! For what? We almost there."

"I said pull the fuck over!" Gotti yelled before placing the handgun to his temple. Turning on the hazard lights, he quickly eased the car over to the sidewalk.

"For some reason, you're starting to make me really nervous. Ever since I came home you've been acting like a real bitch. It makes me feel like if shit gets ugly you gonna run that mouth. From now on don't even open that motherfucker. The boss man only speaks to me from here on out. You ain't about to fuck this opportunity up for me."

As he felt the barrel press into his jaw harder, Clyde closed his eyes and nodded humbly. He put the car back in drive and pulled off so they could complete the mission at hand. The remainder of the ride was driven in complete silence. It didn't take long to reach their destination and the empty street boosted Gotti to handle the issue in a timely fashion. As they pulled in front of the house, he opened the door to step out and snatched the keys from the ignition just in case Clyde began to have any ill feelings.

Gotti threw the hoodie over his head, made his way up to the porch and knocked sternly. After hearing the locks adjust, Juve opened the door and received a solid strike on his chin from Gotti's pistol. Gotti pushed him to the floor and placed a hand over his mouth to assure that he couldn't scream for help.

"One false move and you'll be talking to God in six seconds."

The excruciating pain was thumping through his head and the threat he'd just received caused his movements to cease.

"The money you owe, my boss man. Where is it? And before you speak I'ma warn you about lying. It's not gonna end well," he spat, pulling the hammer back before allowing him to talk.

"This on my life man. I ain't got nothing but fifteen grand in my pocket, that's all. I'm trying my best to get the money to him. I swear," Juve pleaded.

Gotti nearly ripped his jeans off, as he retrieved the large roll of bills and placed it the pocket of his jacket.

"Are you sure it ain't nothin' else I need to know about before I start looking?"

"I wouldn't play with my life like that man."

"Good," Gotti smirked before placing two slugs in the center of his forehead.

Boom! Boom!

He stuffed the gun into his waistline and moved hastily out of the house. After jumping back into the vehicle, Clyde didn't hesitate to pull off. Gotti grabbed the cellphone from the middle console, scanned through the call log and clicked, Bossman.

Chapter 14

Storm sat in the bedroom consuming her third glass of *Grey Goose* while waiting on Dominic to arrive. Since the day she'd bumped into Gotti, alcohol had become her new best friend. That was a silent way to cope with all the drama that had magically appeared during a time that was supposed to be the happiest days of her life. They were still newlyweds, which meant they were supposed to be having non-stop, nasty sex every chance they got. Instead, she was too busy beating ass and dodging a crazy ex that didn't understand it was truly over.

Quickly, becoming agitated with the waiting game she snatched her phone from the nightstand and re-dialed Dominic's number. After several rings, it went to the voicemail.

She huffed as she tossed the phone back to its resting spot. "Dominic, where are you, baby? I need you."

"I'm right here, my love. What's wrong?"

The sound of his baritone voice startled her, sending her heart into a frenzy. "I didn't hear you come in."

"I'm sorry, I didn't mean to frighten you."

Storm stood up and walked into his arms. "I'm so stressed out, I just needed you here with me."

"I'm here now, just tell me what's bothering you."

She rested her head against the lower part of his chest, closed her eyes and contemplated about coming clean. Being that Gotti knowing where they laid their heads it was imperative to tell him, but she was afraid. Fear was something he'd never instilled in her. He always handled her like she was a fragile package. Yet, it was still hard.

"I love you so much, but I think I'm going to mess this up. All I want to be is the perfect wife you want me to be. And it scares me that I won't be able to do that."

Dominic raised Storm's chin, so she could look into his eyes. "Listen to me, perfection is not what I want from you. All I want is for you to be yourself. Your imperfections are what attracted me to you in the first place. That's what makes you special. Self-doubt is your biggest enemy, so don't let that manifest in your mind. If not, you'll kill what we have by the time we reach our one-year anniversary."

Storm's vision became blurry due to the tears that were building up. "I'm sorry, it's just that my past always has a way of interrupting my happiness and I'm allowing it."

"Storm, this is the happiest I've been in my entire life. I want you to understand that. I love you and I will always be honest with you about everything. I promise!"

Dominic placed his hand on her chin and kissed her softly. He always knew the right words to say to pull her out of every slump she fell into. However, the honesty part lingered in her head because she wasn't being truthful with him and he deserved the truth as well.

Suddenly, their kiss came to an abrupt stop. "How much have you had to drink?"

"Umm—I—" she stammered. "Not a lot."

He looked past her and towards the nightstand. The bottle grabbed his attention, so he walked over and picked it up.

Holding it up in the air, he shook his head. "Baby, you drank half of this bottle."

Storm rocked on her heels and played with her fingers, unable to mumble a single word. It was hard to admit that she drinking her pain away.

"I don't know what's truly going on with you, but whatever it is can't be healthy. I'm not going to press you about it. So, whenever you're ready to fill me in, let me know. I just don't want you to become a drunk behind things we can discuss and handle together."

"What do you mean? I told you what's wrong with me. There's nothing else to tell, baby, I swear."

"Storm, you can't possibly think that a man of my caliber is naïve. I was born in the morning, but not this morning, baby. However, I'm going to let it go since you're saying I'm wrong."

The fact that he called Storm out on her bullshit didn't sit too well with her spirit. It was like he saw straight through her soul. She had to be the naïve one to think otherwise.

"Dominic, when I said my vows, I took them seriously. I love you. There is nothing I'm hiding from you." Storm wiped the tears from her eyes. "I don't want to mess this up and I can't lose you."

Dominic pulled her close. "I'm not going anywhere."

The alcohol in Storm's system had her overly emotional and sexually aroused, as she kissed him hard. Aggressively, she unbuckled his belt and pushed him towards the bed.

"I need you so bad, right now." They both shed their clothing and dropped it to the floor. "Sit on the bed."

Dominic obliged and Storm took her place on his lap. Mounting him, she eased down onto his wood and wrapped her arms around his neck. Using his assistance, she rode him with style and grace. The palms of his hands soothed her body, as he touched and teased her flesh.

"Sss—baby, I love you so much," Storm moaned.

"I love you, too!" Dominic gripped the nape of her neck and bit down on the side of it.

"Promise you'll never leave me."

Clenching her vaginal muscles, she rocked her hips harder causing him to damn near bust a premature nut. "Fuck," he grunted. "I promise if you break these vows, I'll kill you."

"Ahh—ooh, put a baby in me."

Dominic remained silent. Holding her by the waist, he stood up. Storm held on tight with her legs around his waist, while he delivered powerful strokes to her kitty. Tears flowed freely down her cheeks when he made her reach a massive orgasm. While her body was in heaven, her heart was bleeding tears in the pits of hell.

After three rounds of non-stop love making the both of them tapped out. Sleep came easy for Storm. Being in her husband's arms all night made her feel safe and secure. The issues at hand disappeared because she was confident that Dominic would never allow anyone to hurt her.

***

The following day, Storm sat on the edge of the bed and watched Dominic get dressed. When it was time for him to put on his tie, she picked it up from beside her and put it on for him.

"You're not going to work today?" he asked, in reference to the robe she was wearing.

"No, I don't feel like it."

"You know it's okay if you put in your two-week notice so you can be a stay at home wife."

Storm stood on her tippy toes and pecked his lips. "I will as soon as I pee on a stick and the test comes back positive."

"Your choice, I have to go, I'll see you later."

Unsatisfied with his answer, she frowned. "Can I ask you a question?"

By that time, Dominic had almost escaped, but he stopped at the door and turned around. "Anything beautiful."

"I mentioned having a baby last night and this morning, but you have yet to respond. Why is that? You don't want to start a family with me?"

"More than anything in this world. I just believe that timing is everything. It will come, just be patient, baby. In the meantime go shopping, so you can see how it feels to spend without working."

"Have a good day." Storm smiled at the thought of having his babies.

"You too."

Two hours later Storm found herself fully dressed and prepared to head out for a day out on the town. Once inside her vehicle, she started it up and backed out of the driveway. The sound of her cell rang through the Bluetooth.

"Hello." There was complete silence on the other end of the receiver. "Hello!" The second time around she turned the volume up on the radio. Plain as day through the speakers was the sound of heavy breathing. Immediately, she grew irritated. "Listen stop playing on my damn phone." After ending the call, she fished around in her purse for her phone. Just as she suspected it was an unknown caller. "This man just don't quit."

Seconds later it started back up and repeated several times. Instead of answering it she let it go to voicemail. After a long drive Storm ended up in the West End. A few blocks from Clark Atlanta University. As she cruised through the neighborhood it brought back so many memories of her relationship with Gotti. The good times and the bad. A faint smile spread across her lips as she reminisced on the days she would leave school just to meet him during her lunch hour to have sex.

Storm pulled up to the stop sign and froze. From a distance, she could see Gotti standing on his grandmother's porch talking on the phone. Suddenly the beating of her heart increased and sweat beads formed on her forehead when he looked in her direction for a split second and turned away.

"Shit!" She shouted while hitting the gas and hooking a right. "Fuck, I hope he didn't see me! Storm why did you come here?" she mumbled.

***

Jade was lying in bed watching television when a call came through. Fear and anxiety massaged her body as she stared aimlessly at the caller I.D. To ignore it would be bad and the consequences would be great. So, using her better judgment she accepted the call.

"H—hello." The shakiness in her voice was a clear indicator that she was afraid.

"What's the plan? You've had more than enough time to put some shit together, so I can get my bitch back," Gotti barked.

"We're not seeing eye to eye, right now. So, it's difficult to get her to listen."

"I don't want to hear no fuckin' excuses. Yo' dumb ass the reason we in this shit, right now. All you had to do was keep your fuckin' mouth shut. Fuck!" He grew irritated quickly. "Who am I kidding? You couldn't keep your legs closed."

"Gotti, you are to blame just as much as I am."

"Fuck all that, you better figure out a way to make this shit happen or they gone find you in the woods with your head cut off!"

Jade stared up at the ceiling, wondering how in the hell she allowed things to get out of hand. The one person she could always count on wanted nothing to do with her and the girls were being shady. Every time she wanted to link up or she called them, they claimed to be busy. If she could go back in time, she would take back the pain she'd caused Storm. Jade closed her eyes and reminisced on the day that changed her friendship forever.

"*Bae, can you please take Jade home for me?*" *Storm whined.*

Gotti shook his head. "*Nah, you do it. That's your homegirl and she looks like she needs you. I'll be right here waiting to finish what you started.*"

"*Fine.*" *Storm sucked her teeth.* "*You know I've been drinking.*"

"*I have, too.*"

"*But you drive better than me.*" *Gotti grinned, but he wasn't budging.* "*Okay, but if I get pulled over and end up in jail that's your fault.*"

He thought about it for a few before responding, "*You lucky, I love you because if not, I wouldn't do it.*" *Gotti stood up and kissed Storm.* "*Be right back.*"

"*Okay! Call me tomorrow, Jade.*"

"*I will, thanks, Gotti.*"

"*Bring yo' ass on. You need to pick better men, too.*"

During the car ride, Gotti didn't say one word. He was too busy rapping. But Jade decided to make small talk anyway.

"*You know you are right.*"

Gotti was hesitant for a good thirty seconds. That led her to believe he didn't want to be bothered.

"*About?*" *he finally said.*

"*Picking better men. It's like I choose the wrong man every time, it never fails.*"

By the time Gotti pulled up in front of Jade's house and put the car in park, she was sobbing loudly.

"*I don't know what's wrong with me. It's like I look at you and I can see that you love, my sister. That's the love I crave. She's lucky to have you.*"

As bad as he wanted her out of the car, he felt bad and engaged in a conversation. "All I can tell you is to let love find you because apparently, you looking in the wrong direction."

The conversation between them lasted an additional five minutes before Gotti brought it to an end. "Hey, I have to go. Take it easy."

"Thanks for listening to me."

"No problem."

Jade leaned over and gave Gotti a hug. When she released her hold on him, she went in for a kiss and slid her hand in his gym shorts. Using his left hand he grabbed her wrist and squeezed it. "What the fuck you doing?"

Jade placed a finger on his lips. "Shh, I just want to sample what I've been hearing about."

Gotti attempted to make her stop, but when he felt her lips wrap around his piece he slid back in the seat and closed his eyes. The Remy had him relaxed and horny, so he went with it. Even though he knew it was wrong, it felt right at the time. The head ultimately led the two of them into the backseat where they engaged in sex.

Jade rolled over onto her side and cried into the pillow. Gotti was right all along, it was her fault that he'd cheated on Storm.

Chapter 15

Dominic pulled up next to Gotti's car, shut off his engine and stepped out. The morning was still young and the meeting for their handled business almost slipped his mind. It was never like Dominic to be late at any time or for any reason. Trying to balance so many things could quickly detour a person, but the objective would always remain firm, no matter the circumstances.

"I see you got here a little early. My apologies for running behind."

"No apology needed. Time is money and you got all the time in the world." Gotti chuckled with a blunt of weed in his mouth.

"I'll take that." Dominic smiled. "You mentioned something about questions. Is there anything you needed to speak on?" he asked with a curious face.

Gotti dug inside his pockets and removed the fifteen thousand dollars tossing it into his hands. "I took that off ya boy last night. Of course, I asked him was anything else in the house. He denied it like all scary ass niggas do when death's knocking. He also claimed he was trying his best to get the cash up for you.

"And then?"

"Then I did what you paid me to do," Gotti said with no emotions for the life he'd just taken.

His issues were way bigger at the time and the money from the job was all he cared about. Tossing the money back, Dominic straightened the jacket to his two-piece suit. Taking blood money was definitely a violation in his rule book. Karma was guaranteed to be a dirty bitch twenty-four-seven and those same tables could easily turn.

"You found that, not me. I'm just making sure the mission was taken care of with no mistakes. Now that we have that understood we can skip to the next subject. Your money, instead of giving me seventeen off every block. You'll bring me twelve, the extra five off each one goes to you. That'll be fifty grand total. Hopefully, that will be enough for y'all services. Is there any reason why Clyde ain't here?"

"Clyde wasn't standing next to me when I pulled my trigger. He waited outside and played the position he was meant to play. There's no purpose for him to hear or see anything dealing with this situation. Leaves less room for any talking. To be frank with you, I don't think he should have any say so at all."

Shrugging his shoulders, Dominic blew off the remark. "It's niggas like Clyde that has given me his loyalty through ups and downs before I was introduced to you. He was the only one staying true with hustling and coming correct. Me not involving him is like saying that I don't need you either. That's not gonna happen. I admit you possess more skills than he does, but all family wasn't meant to be tough and solid like the alpha coming up. Just our presence alone gives us the authority regardless of who's in the front," he stated before shaking his hand.

Preparing to leave, Gotti opened his car door and got inside. He knew that the boss man may have been right about a few of those statements. But a good sounding speech wasn't always about to stop reality from being shown. Power was meant to be used with an iron fist and every question was only meant for one answer. Regardless of whether he respected it or not, shit was about to change.

***

After making it across town to Cleveland Avenue, Gotti pulled inside the South Medical Hospital and made his way towards the entrance. Lately, the stress was at an all-time high, but his actions would always remain the same when it came down to his queen. He stepped through the sliding doors, quickly signed in at the front desk and headed for room number five. When he spotted her bright face, Gotti couldn't help but smile from ear-to-ear. It was clear to everyone that she was his key to life, his most prized possession. No one but Storm could match her pure love and the feeling continued to lift every time he was around her. His grandmother was the only one who could turn that gangsta volume down in his system and turn him back to her sweet and loveable, baby boy.

"Hey, Grandma." He beamed while proceeding over to her side.

"Hey, Granny baby. What are you doing down here so early? I didn't expect to see you until tomorrow."

He placed two warm kisses on her face and sat directly next to her. "You know I wasn't about to stay away, mama. It hurts my heart to see you like this. It's like your health isn't getting any better no matter how much money we run across to pay these people," Gotti explained while holding her frail hand.

"Bless your heart, baby! But you know my almighty God is the giver of all protection and security. This is only a minor stage of my little old life. Just a small tribulation for the greatness that's to come. I thought Storm was going to visit with you. Is she here?"

Sighing deeply, he shook his head. "I've tried to call and tell her mama, but she won't answer any of my calls. I wanted her to visit with me also. I don't think she's happy with my past behavior before I went to prison."

"And that makes you feel a certain way?" she replied while staring into his eyes.

"I mean—no."

"Don't lie to me. I could see the pain written all over your face when you stepped foot into this room. I knew from the moment I met that beautiful girl she would be your rock. She's the only person besides me I've ever seen you show any heart for. How could your leaving just for a few months change that?"

He knew for a fact anything false would never sit well with his grandmother. He refused to fabricate a story just to hide a terrible mistake for himself to look better. No matter how bad it would sound.

"I did something I'm not proud of, mama. I slipped up bad and I cheated on her," he expressed while lowering his vision.

Giving him a disappointed frown, she gently turned his face towards hers. "What would drive you to do something so selfish and hurtful like that, son? She supported you at times when others didn't even want anything to do with you. I didn't raise you to be a womanizer. I've always told you and showed you the way to a woman's heart is through love and honesty. How do you think me, and your grandfather lasted so many years? Even after his death, I refused to date again because he cherished me with a love that was

111

irreplaceable. Life is short, son. I explained the same to your mother before she passed away from this cruel place. It hurts me down to my bones seeing you on this path with your emotions, baby."

"Please don't hurt, mama. I don't want you to be disappointed in me and I can't lose you from stress. You know what the doctor said." Gotti uttered before a tear streamed down his right jaw. "You're all I have left."

"I'm not all you have left. There's a woman in that real world who needs you. But you will never realize that if you're blinded by the streets. You have to face the fact that mama is old now. Complications will happen, but I refuse to let it stop me physically or mentally. I know you wanna make me happy. So, earn your way back into her life and never let her go. You can't let everything slip from your hands because of a mistake. You have to fix it," she said with sternness and a strong grip of the hand.

Wiping his wet face, he placed a kiss on her chunky cheekbone. "I promise, mama. I love you and I will!"

"I love you, too, baby!"

Smiling with satisfaction she hugged his neck and allowed him to leave. As Gotti made his way down the hall, he stopped by the billing department and placed the earned money toward her expensive medical bill. No price was too high when it came to the number one lady in his life. The words of wisdom she poured into him began to touch his soul as he strolled toward the exit of the hospital. By any means necessary, that promise was not going to be broken.

***

Storm sat on the toilet seat praying silently that her dream would come true in the next one hundred and eighty seconds. Her period was seven days late, so there was no doubt in her mind that her mission was complete. Nervousness was at an all-time high, as butterflies flooded her stomach. The thought of having a child growing in her womb made her smile. Storm rubbed the flat surface and continued with the waiting game.

"You can be, Dominic Junior or Reign. It doesn't matter, as long as you're a healthy, baby." The alarm on her cellphone went off, so she closed her eyes and took a deep breath. "Okay, here goes." Storm opened her eyes and grabbed the pregnancy test from the counter. The results displayed on the window shot a dagger straight through her heart. "How can I not be pregnant? This has to be wrong."

She grabbed her cellphone and searched through her contacts until she came across Dr. Solomon's number.

"Good afternoon, Storm. To what do I owe the pleasure of this call?" he said.

"Hey, I need to see you soon. Can I come by the office really quick please?"

The urgency in her voice caused great concern. "Is everything okay?"

"My cycle is seven days late. I took a test, but it came back negative. I just want to be sure."

"I mean that's natural, but if it would make you feel better we can do some blood work."

"Yes, please."

"How fast can you get here?"

"Twenty minutes."

"Come on."

"Thank you so much, I really appreciate this."

"You're welcome."

Storm arrived at the office in exactly twenty minutes. This was the moment of truth and she wanted answers. The waiting area was empty so she walked right up to the counter.

"Hey, Storm."

"Hi, Janet."

"Come straight back, Dr. Solomon is waiting on you."

Storm rushed to the back and stepped into the office where the doctor was sitting at her desk. The sound of footsteps caused her to swivel towards the door.

"Well, that was fast. Did Mr. Dominic buy you a private jet?"

For the first time, that day Storm giggled. "I wish."

Dr. Solomon grabbed a cup from the counter and passed it to her. "Fill this up for me."

"Okay."

It took all of three minutes for her to use the restroom and return. Storm sat the hot cup of pee on the desk. Dr. Solomon put on a pair of gloves and did the test while she watched closely. Storm paced the floor anxiously with her hands in her pockets. Finally, the results were ready.

The doctor turned the chair in her direction so she could face her. A pregnant pause filled the room and Storm's heart was pumping hard and fast, while she rubbed her hands together.

Then she broke the silence. "Give it to me straight. What does it say?"

"I'm sorry, Storm. I know how bad you want this baby."

Storm held her head back to keep from breaking down. Over the years the two women established a solid bond. They considered themselves as friends, which was why she was able to come in on such short notice.

Dr. Solomon stood up and pulled Storm into her arms. "Don't cry, you're still young. It will happen when the time is right."

Storm tried to laugh to keep from crying. "You sound like, Dominic."

"That's a smart man."

"I just want to be a mother. Is that too much to ask?"

The doctor let her go. "No, it's not and you will be one sooner or later. Just stay in prayer and continue to practice. In the Bible, Sarah didn't have her first child until age ninety-nine."

Storm laughed it off. "I don't want to be that damn old bearing a child. Who's going to run behind him or her? Definitely not me."

"The lesson is to have patience, my dear. In the meantime, I am going to prescribe you some birth control pills."

"I'm trying to have a baby."

"I know, This will regulate your cycle and increase your chances at getting pregnant. Take it for a few weeks, then stop. Track your cycle, so you will know when your ovulation days are."

"Okay, I can do that."

114

"Download the Flo app and log your last period. Then when this one comes log that as well, stay on top of that."

"I will, thanks so much."

"You're quite welcome, darling. Before you go I want to draw your blood and test it."

"Alright." Storm sat down on the table and waited to be poked. Things didn't turn out the way she wanted, but with a solid plan in place, she would be having a baby sooner, rather than later.

Chapter 16
One week later

"Heyyyy thunder, thots. What's going on?" Kendra sang as she walked up to the table to join the ladies for lunch at The Sundial Restaurant.

"Girl, bye," Storm waved her off. "Y'all friend was the only thot in the clique."

"Let the pettiness begin," Tia replied and sipped her Hurricane.

"I digress." Kendra held her hand up. "Jade seems really apologetic."

"Yeah, I bet." Storm gave her the side eye.

"Seriously. She called me today because she wanted to go out for drinks, but I told her I was meeting up with you. So, you know how that went."

"I'm not going there today."

"Good," Tia added. "So, Storm, what's new? How is Paradise Island? It's been a minute since we last hung out."

"Yes, please fill us in on the interesting details of your perfect life."

"We're not perfect, Ken."

"Damn near," Kendra contested.

"We're just compatible. We bring out the best in each other." Storm twirled the flawless wedding ring on her finger and smiled, it felt good to be the luckiest woman in the world. Everything about him screamed perfection and he was all hers. Now only if she could get pregnant soon, she'd be complete.

"Why are you cheesing so hard?" Tia smirked.

Storm was filled with glee as she spoke highly of her prince charming. "Y'all just don't understand how much that man means to me. How much I love him. I swear he came in my life at the perfect time. Dominic was a breath of fresh air after all the bullshit I went through with, Gotti."

As Storm continued to pour her heart out, she turned to face Kendra. "He is everything I ever wanted in a man, and I have you to thank for that. If you would've never pulled me out of the house that night, I wouldn't have such a great man in my life."

"You're welcome. So does that mean you're not going to meet up with him and listen to his side of the story?"

Storm gave Kendra the side eye and kicked her leg underneath the table. "What?"

Tia put her elbows on the table and leaned forward. "Well, when is this supposed to happen, because I'm in the dark about this treacherous ass plan?"

"I never said I was going to do it." Storm nodded her head in Kendra's direction. "She seems to think I should have a sit down with, Gotti, so he can tell his side of the story."

"For what? That's a thing of the past. Y'all not getting back together, so it doesn't matter at this point. You're a married woman now, and Jade told you all you need to know. Let sleeping dogs lie."

"That's what I was thinking, too. But at the same time, I want to know what happened and why he did it. Everyone at this table knows how I feel about him. I spent years with that man."

"Don't you mean *felt*? Like past tense because what you're saying sounds like the present to me." Tia needed confirmation that her ears weren't playing tricks on her.

"You heard what she said," Kendra added. "And that's why I told her to go, she needs closure."

Tia had a different take on things. "Well, I don't think that's a good idea. She does not need to meet up with him period. All that's going to do is cause old ass feelings to resurface and it's too late to apologize. She needs to carry on with her life and be happy with the man she walked down the aisle with."

"Can y'all stop talking like I'm not sitting, right here?" Storm pushed her plate to the center of the table. Her appetite was completely shot. "This is too much to deal with."

"No it's not, ignore his ass. Don't let him get out and disrupt your life." Tia was always ready to snap.

"She could've if you didn't send her that picture of him. Now she all hot and bothered cause she wanna smash."

"First of all ma'am, I didn't know that would cause a problem. I was only trying to see if she knew he was out. It ain't my fault he fine as fuck." Tia could no longer hold in her laughter, but Storm didn't think it was a laughing matter.

"Yeah, laugh at my pain! This is serious and y'all playing."

Kendra rubbed Storm's shoulder. "Sorry, boo, we just trying to lighten the mood."

Tia tapped her fork against the glass. "Okay, on a serious note. Do you wanna fuck him? Like is that what you need to do in order to get him out of your system?"

Storm shrugged her shoulders. "I—I don't know what it is. I love, Dominic, and I will never leave him."

"But what, you'll still fuck, Gotti? I already know it's coming so spill it," Tia chimed in before she could finish her sentence.

"I still have love for, Gotti, but I'm not in love with him. If that makes sense? I know he did me wrong by fucking, Jade. I get it, and for that reason alone, I will never forgive him. But when I saw him, I started reminiscing about the past, when things were good." Storm looked away and a single tear cascaded down her cheek. Moments later a stream of tears followed.

That was her moment of truth and she didn't care how anyone felt about it. Just as Kendra was about to reach for Storm, Tia shook her head, so she could breathe in peace.

"I loved him with everything in me and he betrayed me in the worst way. I'm just so mad with him. I was everything that I promised to be and he still fucked up. While he sat in the county waiting for his trial, I was there. During his bid, I was there. All I did was work, go home and wait on his calls night and day. True enough I was lonely, but I kept my word and didn't fuck another man. Gotti was my first and was supposed to be my only."

For the first time, Kendra and Tia didn't open their mouths. Instead, they allowed her to vent and get her emotions in check. So, that she wouldn't take home any dead weight in her heart. Storm used a napkin from the table to clean her face. Once it was dry, she turned back to face them.

"I know y'all think I'm stupid for crying over him when I have a husband at home, but this is how I feel. Feelings don't evaporate overnight, and we have history. Truthfully, I just want to confront him about it and look him in the eyes, so I can see the truth. I swear I don't want him back."

Tia sat quietly trying to get her words together. Watching her best friend in pain didn't feel good. So, she wanted to make sure she wasn't being insensitive. Truthfully, she understood where she was coming from so that should've made the conversation a little easier to deal with.

"We've all been down this road before with no good ass exes. The only difference is we're not married. So, no I don't think you're stupid and you have the right to ask questions. The two people that you loved the most betrayed you and did the unthinkable. It makes sense that you're hurting just don't ruin your marriage behind it."

"Thanks, T, for understanding. That means so much to me to have the support of my friends, my real sisters."

"You're welcome, girl. That's what we're here for."

Kendra picked up her Margarita and took a long swig from the straw. During Storm's confessional, all she did was take shots. So, she was tipsy as hell.

"You got that right and I say if you want to fuck him, do it. Shit, I know I would. Just don't get sprung though because you know he gone fuck the air, shit and piss out of your ass." Kendra was slurring her ass off and rocking side to side.

"Put that glass down drunky, old bad, advice giving ass. I swear you crazy," Tia teased. "She wants closure, not dick."

"Nah she definitely want dick, dick."

Storm laughed at Kendra's comment. "He does have dick for days, but my husband does, too. So, yeah, I'm not in need of that and my baby definitely lays it down every night."

"Well, alright, I guess you heard that, Ken." Tia giggled.

"Child, I did."

The waiter walked over to the table. "Can I get something else for you ladies?"

Kendra didn't hesitate to answer that question. "Hell, yeah, bring us ten shots of Tequila."

"Ten shots, Ken, really?" Tia shook her head.

"Yes, Storm needs at least three of them."

"I do."

"Well, shit let's run it then." Tia danced in her seat. "It's the weekend, turn up.

"Damn right." Kendra looked at the waiter. "Bring that order back, stat."

The girls laughed when he walked off. Storm laughed the hardest. "You stupid. We are not at work for you to be saying stat, fool."

"He knew what I meant, though."

"For real, for real. He hauled ass from over here." Storm's phone vibrated hard against the table. She grabbed it and read the message from Dominic.

Love of my Life//: I'll be home late tonight. Keep it warm for me.

My world//: Work stuff?

Love of my Life//: Yes, that's the only thing that will make me late when it comes to you.

My World//: I love you so much!

Love of my Life//: I love you! Enjoy your outing with the girls. See you later!

My World//: Later baby!

"Who you texting, Gotti." Kendra leaned over peeking at her phone.

"Dominic."

"Oh."

"Here are your shots ladies." The waiter placed all of the shot glasses in a straight line. "Enjoy."

"Oh, we certainly will." Kendra grabbed the first glass and took it straight to the head. Tia and Storm were staring at her. "What? Y'all asses better drink up and I'm paying for all this."

"I'm on your ass." Storm picked up one and did the same thing, followed by Tia. "We gone be fucked up messing with you."

"Good, life is too short to be sad and miserable. We supposed to be living our best life, right now and that's what we gon' do." Kendra took another shot.

For the next hour the girls got wasted and during that time Storm's phone continued to ring constantly. It was Gotti. His text message confirmed it.

//: *Storm please answer, it's Gotti, baby. I need you!*

The first thing on her mind was to respond, but she changed her mind quickly. Now wasn't the time to confront him about his past indiscretion.

"How did he get my number?" she mumbled under her breath, so they couldn't hear what she was saying.

There was only one logical explanation for his calls and that was to get her back. The only person that could have given Gotti her number was slimy ass, Jade. Storm dropped her phone into her purse and continued with the turn-up session.

Chapter 17

The terrible moment of reality was now starting to kick in hard with Gotti losing his grandmother. He never envisioned leaving her hospital room only to get a call hours later that she was gone. The heart he carried inside his chest felt as though it was snatched out and buried in a pit of fire. Her love was the glue that kept his mind frame from falling to pieces. There was no such thing as life without her. Picking up his cellphone from the bathroom counter, he tried to reach Storm for the tenth time. The funeral was nearly over and he couldn't even get a text message or call in return to explain his reasoning.

"Yo' cuz, it's about that time. Everybody's leaving out of the church so we can make it to the burial site on time," Clyde said, as he stepped through the door.

Using a hand to wipe his tears, he turned around with a fixed look of hostility.

"You a'ight?" Clyde asked.

"Do it look like, I'm okay?"

Knowing that it was a rhetorical question, he decided to switch the conversation. "I understand, I wanted to let you know that I spoke to Bossman this morning. He's gonna give us a bigger supply in the next few weeks so things are looking to get better with our business."

Gotti clutched the bridge of his nose and started slowly gritting his teeth in anger. "My grandmother is laying in a fucking casket and you got the nerve to talk about some bullshit like this."

"I was just giving you the heads up about what's going on. It ain't like you been caring about nothing else," he mumbled before turning to leave.

Gotti caught the slick remark, grabbed the back of his shirt collar and pushed him forcefully into the wall. Then he pulled the handgun from his waist and placed it to the bottom of his chin.

"The only reason I'm sparing you is because of mama. I'm like two minutes from blowing yo' shit back. If you wanna live put ya mouth in ya ass and tape it up."

Gotti took his silence as understanding, pushed him to the floor and tucked the pistol back in his pants. Gotti buttoned up his suit jacket and headed out of the bathroom.

* * *

The drive to the cemetery was beyond exhausting. Arguments between close family members were stirring by the second and the intense conflict caused Gotti to drift into his own miserable world. His mind started reflecting to his mother when he was younger. Their rough relationship placed a veil over his heart making it impossible for him to care about anything. He would never be nothing in her eyes, but it surely wasn't the same when it came down to, Big Mama. No matter how bad or destructive he became, she always catered to him and told everyone the same statement.

"He's just expressing himself the way he knows how. That'll be my baby until the end of time."

Her words always seemed to land on deaf ears because the hatred continued to grow within the family towards him. The lousy support was the same reason he decided to devote his love to the streets. Hearing the preacher call his name, he broke out of the tranquil state and realized it was time to speak on his grandmother's behalf. Standing from the pew, he placed the white rose on her casket before clearing his throat and facing the crowd.

"I'm not gonna hold everyone up too long because out of everyone I truly want mama to rest in peace. I've spent nearly my whole life hearing that I was a disgrace to this family. That I deserve to be in prison forever. Even dead, but it seems my queen didn't feel the same way. She was actually the only one who believed that I had a golden heart inside of me. That I could actually be the one to leave a legacy for my generation. Now that I'm grown, I understand what she meant. It's because I'm firm. Because I would do whatever it takes to feed my own. Today's my mama's funeral and instead of you all being firm you motherfuckers argued and made this day even worse for the ones who actually care. If it's not too much to ask, please just put a rose on the casket and leave," he spat before the tears started pouring down his face.

After two long hours passed, Gotti sat in front of his grandmother's grave alone and tried to drink away his pain with a bottle of Hennessy. The light rain that drizzled across her casket only made things more depressing. He pulled out his iPhone and dialed Storm's number. After a few rings, her sweet voice came through the line causing his heart pace to speed up.

"Hello?"

"Why aren't you answering my calls? I've called you a hundred times this week.

"Gotti, why are you calling me? I thought I explained to you that I'm married. There's a reason you're not getting an answer," she said with frustration.

"Please, ma, I need you next to me, right now. I don't wanna argue. Can you come meet me?"

"You don't need me because if you did, you wouldn't have done spiteful things to break my heart. So, no, I cannot meet you," she huffed before hanging up.

Redialing her number, he received the voicemail indicating that she forwarded his call. "You don't fucking love me!" he shouted before pulling the gun from his pants and placing it to his temple.

Gotti snapped a picture in front of his grandmother's grave for proof. After sending the photo to Storm, he decided to take his last drink and end it all for good. Nothing would ever be the same without his world. It was pointless to even continue on with life. Just as he placed a bullet into the chamber, his phone began to vibrate. Viewing her number, he paused before answering.

"What, I thought you didn't wanna talk to me?"

"Why are you at the cemetery with a gun to your head? What's going on?"

"Maybe if you would have picked up the phone last week. I could have told you that my grandmother died. But that ain't important. Nothing but your marriage matters, remember!"

"Oh, my God, Gotti I'm sorry. I didn't—"

"You didn't care. I told you I needed your help. You promised me you wouldn't leave, and you would be here for me if this ever happened. Fuck everybody!" he shouted. "After I blow my brains out maybe you can make it to my funeral and say your last goodbyes before they put me in the fucking ground."

"Don't say things like that. I'm sorry about you losing your Grandmother, but you've made mistakes that placed us in this position, Gotti. I wouldn't have hesitated to come to the funeral and show my respect, but things have changed for me and you," she stressed with worry.

"If you're not coming there's no reason to keep wasting your breath. I got a date with death and you just wanna talk me out of it."

"I know you truly care for me and you wouldn't make me choose between hurting my husband, and standing beside you. I can't handle this type of pressure, Gotti. Don't you understand that?"

"Well fuck him and fuck you, too," he raged before releasing a shot into the air.

Hearing the loud bang Storm let out a shrill scream. "Gotti! Hello, Gotti!"

Launching his phone into the air, he dropped to his knees before breaking down in tears.

***

Storm couldn't believe what she'd just heard. Her hands trembled as she called him back repeatedly. However, she had no luck getting him on the line. Immediately she leaped from the bed but had to pause because the many shots she took rushed to her head. She grabbed a hold of the nightstand.

"Slow it down, you fucked up, right now."

Storm slipped her feet into her sandals, then grabbed her purse and keys so she could make sure he was okay. It was the least she could do.

Storm made her way into the cemetery that she knew all too well. She drove slowly down the path in search of a freshly dug grave. It didn't take long before she spotted Gotti lying next to it.

Trepidation settled in as she struggled to change gears. "God, please don't let him be dead."

Storm emerged quickly from the truck and ran at a high rate of speed through the low cut grass. If he'd taken his own life she would never forgive herself for not coming to his aide fast enough.

"*Gotti! Gotti!*" Storm screamed, as she dropped to her knees beside him and placed her hand on his shoulder.

When he looked up at her his eyes were bloodshot red and his face was moist from his tears. Gotti was never the emotional type, so to see him like that created a soft spot in her heart.

"I'm so sorry, for your loss." Storm pulled him up by his arms and embraced him.

Gotti squeezed her tight and closed his eyes. The scent of her favorite perfume filled his nostrils. "Thank you for coming—I love you, so much, Storm. I'm sorry for everything I ever did wrong to you. But that shit with, Jade, was bogus as fuck and wasn't my fault."

Hearing her name roll off his tongue made her cringe and pull away from him instantly. "When are you going to take responsibility for your own actions?"

"If I initiated that shit I would say it, but I didn't. Straight out the gate, I knew she wasn't a real friend. That hoe wanted your spot and I told you that."

"You owed me your loyalty. No one else, I was your woman Gotti. You betrayed me with someone I considered a sister."

"She been foul, and I told you I didn't want to take her home."

"That didn't mean you had to fuck her." Storm became choked up thinking back to that night.

Gotti could see that she was attempting to get up, so he pulled her close to him. "Please don't leave me, I need you and I fucked up."

Taking a deep breath, he stared at Big Mama's final resting place and wiped his right eye. It was like she was watching him and reciting her final words to him once again. This was his chance to make things right, so he took advantage of that moment.

"That night you asked me to take her home. I didn't want to, but you kept on pushing. There was something about her aura that didn't sit well with me. She was crying in the car and wanted to talk. I gave her some sound advice and told her that I had to go—" Gotti paused so he could look her in her eyes when he revealed her fake friend. "She leaned over and hugged me, then grabbed my dick. I gripped her wrist so she could stop."

Storm bit down on her bottom lip because she couldn't believe what she was hearing. As bad as she wanted to say something, she remained silent. It was the confession she had been waiting for.

"That bitch told me she wanted to sample what she'd been hearing about from you. So, that let me know you were telling her about our sex life, that was your first mistake. You don't tell your girls everything we do behind closed doors."

Gotti was absolutely right and she knew that, but she would've never expected that from Jade. Now it all made sense why Jade didn't elaborate on the details of that night. She made it seem as if it was something they agreed to do and not like she seduced him while he was under the influence of alcohol.

For the next minute or so, no one uttered a single word. They only looked at each other. Old memories of her and Gotti sitting at his mother's grave when they were madly in love resurfaced. Suddenly, Gotti leaned towards Storm and kissed her softly on the lips. Storm placed her hand on his chest to push him away, but he refused to let go and gripped her tighter.

Being on familiar territory increased the sexual chemistry between the old lovers. Smacking of their lips and light moans were all that could be heard. As Storm leaned back in his arms, he pulled her on top of him and caressed her body. In his mind Storm belonged to him and he was determined to get her back by any means necessary. Sex would definitely open that door. Once she let him between her legs, her heart was guaranteed to follow.

"Gotti stop." Storm pulled away from him. "I have to go."

"You leaving me?"

"You're okay now, I need to get back home."

"Okay, that's fair." He stroked the left side of her face. "I'm staying at a hotel a few blocks from here so can you follow me, please? Just to make sure I get there in one piece."

"Sure, come on." She agreed.

Chapter 18

Once they arrived downtown, Storm pulled into the Hilton hotel directly behind Gotti. As she patiently watched him park the car sideways, she shook her head knowing that he was above the normal drinking limit. It was difficult to see him take in his grandmother's death and by observing his actions and emotions alone, began to make her feel sorry for him.

Gotti climbed out of his vehicle and staggered over to her passenger side window. "I guess this is goodbye. If I don't make it through tonight. You can tell everyone I said fuck them and kick rocks until their fucking feet break," he slurred while shooting a middle finger.

The dry tears on his face showed that he had been crying the entire way. His appearance was a disaster and it was probably guaranteed that he would end up in a jail cell before the night was over, maybe even a casket. As he stumbled towards the entrance. He crashed to the ground causing her to jump out of the car.

"Oh, my God, Gotti, you're going to kill yourself. You need to go to the hospital," she sighed with worry before helping him up to his feet.

Wrapping one arm around her shoulder, he held his bottle of Hennessy for dear life. "Fuck a hospital. They can't bring you and my mama back!" he shouted causing a few citizens in the parking lot to look their way.

"Stop yelling! Drinking will only make things worse. And you're not in the right mind to have a gun. You're going to get in more trouble if you don't get some rest." She advised before walking him through the door of the hotel.

As she helped him move across the lobby, she placed his back against the wall by the elevators. "What floor is your room on?"

"Eighty-eight," he mumbled before putting the bottle back to his lips.

"Gotti, this building doesn't have eighty-eight floors."

Remembering that he wasn't stable, she dug into his pocket and pulled out the key card. She was thankful the number was printed on the side. The silver doors to the elevator opened.

"How could you get married on me?" he asked while she guided him inside.

"Gotti, please, I didn't destroy our relationship, and this isn't the time to talk about that."

"I never meant to hurt you, so stop saying that shit." He mugged, laying his head on her shoulder.

Knowing he was liable to flip at any second, she remained quiet until reaching the eighth floor. '*Dominic would kill me if he could see this, right now,*' she thought before stopping in front of his room door.

Sliding the card through the slot, the locks clicked allowing them to enter. The cold breeze from the A.C. instantly connected with her flesh, as they stepped across the threshold letting the door close behind them.

"I would advise you not to leave this room tonight. Take a shower and get some sleep," Storm warned, as she began removing his suit discarding it across the floor.

"Thank you." He opened his arms indicating that he wanted a hug.

Storm paused for a second before reacting and embracing him. The scent of his Y.S.L cologne teased her nose, as her head met his solid chest. Sensing her comfortable aura, he slowly slid his hands down her back until he gripped her voluptuous backside through the thin Valentino Garavani dress.

"Gotti stop," she mumbled when he placed his lips on her neck. The tingle between her legs sparked faster than a campfire, as she tried to back away from his touch.

Gotti locked a firm grasp around her waist to keep her still, his tongue swirled to the opposite side applying the same affection.

"Gotti, pleaseee stop," Storm begged feeling his pole rise through his shorts.

Gotti swiftly picked her up and balanced her against the wall. "Fuck that, you ain't never denied me and you ain't about to start now," Gotti said with slanted eyes before locking a hand around her throat. Then he reached down dropped his shorts, stroked his large piece and slid her panties to the side.

"Nooo, I told you, I'm married! Gotti, I can't do this." Storm jerked back and forth with tears at the corner of her eyes.

Gotti ignored her pleas and guided his dick into her slippery slit, forcing himself inside her, making her gasp for air. Her heart felt as if it was about to stop as he began to land hard strokes between her soft pussy lips. Storm struggled to release her words as Gotti cuffed her ass and dug deeper while nibbling on the crease of her chest.

"Tell me you love me." Fighting hard to deny the truth, she bit her bottom lip and closed her eyes. Storm hoped he wouldn't ask her that again. He speeded his pace and repeated himself. "Tell me you still love me, Storm!"

His dick game began to make her kitty gush forth in excitement. After her first orgasm released, she melted and wrapped her arms around his neck. "I love you," she moaned.

Pleased with her answer, he carried her over to the bed and gently laid her down. "Turn that ass over."

The intoxicating sex made her comply and turn over on all fours. As he looked down at her bubble ass glowing like a full moon, he eased back into her honeypot. The sight of Storm's face balling up from his length added excitement.

Gotti slammed a hand down across her right cheek. "You can't take what's mine. You hear me?" he grunted plunging in her tight walls.

"Yes! I hear you—I hear you," she whined from the rough passion he was releasing.

Gotti grinned while watching her ass clap against his midsection. This was the moment he'd waited for throughout his entire bid. He delivered hard thrusts for the next five minutes and spilled his orgasm deep inside of her. After resting on her back for a few seconds, Gotti kissed her shoulder and stood up.

"No! No! No!" she screamed into the sheets before turning over and standing on her feet with a hand over her mouth. "I have to get home."

He grabbed her waist. "Just stay, I need you here with me tonight."

"Please, Gotti, I've already gone too far. I have to go!" She pushed past him and slid on her sandals.

As she quickly exited the room, she didn't bother looking back and took the elevator back to the first floor. "You're so fucking weak," Storm mumbled to herself before straightening her hair.

She folded her arms, walked toward the entrance and froze from the eyes that beamed directly at her.

"Ms. Motherfucking Sneaky, what are you doing here bitch?" Stumbling on her reply, she reversed the question. "Tia, what the hell are you doing here?"

"I just dropped my little cousin off upstairs for her sleepover and you look like you just had some dick dropped deep in yo' guts." She smirked.

"No, I just came in to use the bathroom."

"Bitch, I was standing in the lobby when you carried, Gotti upstairs. Spill the juice. Did his dick get bigger?" Tia asked with a devilish smile.

"Tia stop! Don't do this to me, right now."

"You dirty little freak. You gave up that ass, didn't you? Shit, the least you could've done was recorded it so I could see."

Strom buried her face into her hands to shake away the nasty replay of Gotti giving her the business. "Please don't say anything, Tia."

"Tia—who is that ma'am? I think you got the wrong woman because I've never seen you before." She laughed before grabbing one of her nipples and walking off.

"Shit!" She cursed quietly while making her way out of the hotel. She climbed into her car and pulled away hastily hoping her engine could beat him home.

* * *

As she turned down her street, she thanked God Dominic had yet to arrive home. Storm turned off the truck and rushed inside, making a beeline to the kitchen. She opened a bottle of Remy Martin VSOP, poured herself a glass and downed it. While taking several deep breaths, she headed upstairs to their master bedroom and entered the bathroom. Storm cut on the shower and shed her clothing. After the steam began to fill the glass walls, she stepped in and placed her head underneath the sprinkler.

The hot water splashed hard against her skin, opening up her pores. It was going to take more than a shower to remove the dirt she'd just done. Dominic warned her that if she broke her vows, he would kill her. They weren't married ninety days before she fucked up. Sadly, she spoke that into existence the night she cried in his arms. Storm knew Gotti was her weakness and vice versa. Sleeping with Gotti was a terrible mistake and only the man upstairs knew what was about to transpire. Storm had officially opened that door once again, even though she knew he wanted her back and wasn't about to let her go without a fight.

Every negative outcome played in her mind. If Dominic even caught a whiff of her infidelity she might as well commit suicide. Tears welled up in her eyes and blended with the water. How could she lay beside the man she vowed to love and cherish forever knowing she let another man into her husband's sacred place?

"And you told him you loved him. How stupid can you be? Not to mention he fucked your old best friend and ruined everything. Storm, you fucking up already."

After lathering up her loofa, she scrubbed her skin roughly until her skin was tender. Every speck of Gotti needed to be scrubbed completely off her body. Too bad she wasn't bathing in holy water, so she could start fresh. Finally, she was done conducting her own baptism and got out of the shower. Dominic being out late was a blessing in disguise. That would allow her to go to sleep to keep from facing him.

Storm dried herself off and tossed her towel on the foot of the bed. Then grabbed the lotion from the dresser, bent over and rubbed her legs.

"Hell, yeah, keep that ass just like that." Dominic walked up and palmed her backside. "You must've felt my presence."

Wind got caught in her throat causing her to cough. Having sex was not a part of the plan. "Hey, baby, I didn't hear you come in."

Dominic was so close that she could feel his rod poking her through his slacks. The sound of his belt buckle followed before she heard them hit the floor. Storm continued to lotion the same spot just to kill time. She had never slept with two men concurrently, let alone in the same night and hours apart.

'*For sure he'll know I just finished fuckin'*,' she thought to herself.

The warmth of his hands going up and down her back sent chills down her spine, but he didn't stop there. Dominic's hand anxiously found its way to the center. Slowly, he rubbed her clit. Once he felt moisture on his fingertips, he slipped two fingers inside, pulling them in and out.

Storm couldn't deny him, so she went along with it and prayed he wouldn't notice the difference. Arching her back, she held the footboard and propped one leg on the mattress. Seconds later she could feel Dominic's rod spread her lips and fill her up. Her kitty griped him as it normally did, so a sigh of relief came over her. Happy she was home free, she threw it back on him and closed her eyes. Aggressively he beat the box and smacked her ass repeatedly, making it jiggle.

"Sss—oohhh—ooh!" Storm gripped the sheets and held her breath. The constant stabbing made the bottom of her stomach hurt giving her an instant flashback of the way Gotti put the dick down not too long ago.

"This pussy belongs to me," he grunted.

She was in another world, as she moaned. "Ooh, Gotti, damn!"

"What you said?" Dominic questioned.

It was at that moment when she realized she'd had a slip of the tongue. "Ooh, got damn." She lied.

Dominic gripped her hips and leaned forward while planting soft kisses on her back. "Lay on your back and open your legs."

Without hesitation, she complied. Dominic positioned himself between her legs, placed one of them onto his shoulder and slid back in. The guilt was riding her hard, as he stroked her inner core with

134

slow grinds. Gotti's words played over in her mind like a broken record.

"Tell me you still love me, Storm. You can't take what's mine. You hear me?"

Her mind was playing tricks on her because some Freaky Friday shit went down. When she looked into Dominic's eyes, all she could see was Gotti's face and hear his voice.

"I love you, Storm and I'll never let you go."

Before she told on herself, she clenched her eyes tight and looked away. Twenty minutes later, Dominic finally reached his peak, laid down beside Storm and wrapped his arms around her waist.

"Everything okay? You seemed distant tonight."

"Yes, baby." Storm kissed his lips. "I'm just tired, I had too many shots with the girls."

Dominic laughed. "Now you know Kendra can drink you under the table. You lightweight."

"Yeah, she set my ass up."

Storm laid underneath Dominic all night and watched him sleep. "How could I do that to a man that's so perfect? One that does everything for me and is faithful?"

Sleep didn't come easy that night and she spent the rest of it in and out of consciousness. Like her father had always told her, *"There is no rest for the wicked."*

Now she finally understood what he meant.

Chapter 19
Six Weeks Later

As he strolled through Lennox mall with his young shooter, Gotti purchased every piece of new designer clothing he spotted. Tonight was his private party at the club. Not only to kick shit but to announce the start of his new movement. Within the past month, his checks were rising and the reputation was poppin' around half of the city. After spreading his young team around the neighborhoods, he began to set up shop.

The local hood niggas couldn't respect the way he barged in on every block, snatching territory as if he owned Atlanta. Shortly after his crew's body count started to stack, men bowed down for the new rules Gotti was trying to enforce.

"I ain't gone even lie, I gotta be tight sliding in that motherfucker tonight. All these bad bitches about to be in the building. I'm smashing at least three and drinking until I pass the fuck out."

Ignoring him, Gotti continued to count the bills to pay for his merchandise at the register.

"I hope you ain't about to be on that stiff mean shit all through the night. Ain't no hoe trying to bust it for you with that nonchalant act my guy."

Gotti swiveled his neck in his direction with a look so sharp, it could have easily slit his throat. "Nigga, do I look like I give a fuck about a nasty ass freak bitch. If stupid ass young fools like you knew how to keep some paper in ya' pocket. You probably could get you a dime piece and a mansion. Instead, you settle for crumbs and thots."

"What's wrong with the thots, Gotti? Everybody don't want no uptight, bougie ass bitch. We getting money now. I don't give a damn about no mansion, big bro."

"Exactly. That's what makes niggas in the world differently. I'm not with stunting for just the moment. I need the whole state at my feet, so I can do what I please. This is the reason I'm calling everybody out tonight. All that petty broke minded shit will have no room on my team. We strictly 'bout business."

Gotti pushed his finger against his young shooter's head. "Log that shit in your memory. Put the rest of that miscellaneous trash in a box, tape it up and mail that shit off to Africa with no return address," he said sternly while grabbing his bags.

"I'm always about my business period. I'm just saying ain't nothing wrong with having some fun, my nigga. You gotta start living life and slash that serial killer mentality, bro." He chuckled.

"Can you please shut the fuck up!"

Before Trel could reply, Gotti froze with a stale look as if he was being robbed. The bags in his hands hit the floor as he took a small step forward. Blinking twice, he knew his eyes weren't deceiving him. The sight of Dominic holding hands with Storm snatched the air out of his entire body. He watched as they shared a laugh and she leaned in for a passionate kiss crumbling his heart to pieces. "This pussy motherfucker!" he mumbled feeling the rage pump through his chest.

Following Gotti's eyes, Trel spotted what held his attention. "Ain't that yo girl, bro?"

The thought of killing them both slid through his brain until he remembered they were standing in the middle of an overcrowded mall. "I been working for this hoe ass nigga since I came home and he was busting my bitch the whole time."

"What? Give me the word, big bro. I'll take care of that boy ass, right now." Trel offered clutching the handle of his gun.

As he watched them disappear inside the Gucci outlet, he retrieved his bags. "Not here, I'ma handle that bitch personally. You can bet that. Let's get the fuck out of here," he spat watching Storm's happy expression through the window.

* * *

Thirty minutes later, Gotti was swerving his Dodge Demon in front of Clyde's home. "You want me to come with you?"

"Nah, lil' nigga, I got this shit. Just keep the car running." He climbed out and jogged through the lawn until he reached the front porch.

After pounding on the door with the side of his fist for a minute too long, Clyde answered with a bewildered expression on his face. "Why the hell you knocking like the cops? I got all types of shit sitting out man."

Gotti landed a solid punch to his right eye, causing his body to crash to the floor. "You a real snake ass nigga. I knew you was gonna give me a reason to hurt you after I spared your dumb ass on the strength of, my mama."

Clyde rolled onto his side, touching the side of his face that was starting to swell horribly. "What the fuck are you talking about?"

"You thought I wasn't gonna find out? You introduced me to this fake ass plug who running around the city with, my girl!" Gotti yelled landing another blow to the side of his chin.

Clyde scurried to his feet, rushed for his legs, lifted him in the air and rammed his back against the living room wall. The pistol fell from his waist hitting the hardwood floor.

Gotti shot Clyde a sharp uppercut and stepped back throwing up his guard. "Run up, fuck nigga!"

Clyde knew he was no match to his cousin's strength, but he couldn't bow down. He swung a wild overhand and received a hard hook that shattered his jaw on impact.

Gotti grabbed the back of his head and rammed a vicious knee into his nose. "Get up!"

The blood that was pouring from Clyde's nose caused his eyes to tear up from the brutal beating he was receiving. An attempt to cover his face was pointless after Gotti started to kick him numerous times in the back and head. Quickly maneuvering over to his Ruger 9mm handgun, Gotti cocked a bullet into the chamber and placed it swiftly into Clyde's mouth.

"*Wait—wait*! Nigga, I'm your cousin. Why would I lie to you about some shit like that? We family," he begged through a slurred speech.

Gotti's eyes were menacing and cold. Clyde could feel his life flash as the barrel touched his skin. "Nigga, my mama is dead and gone. Family don't exist in my world if it ain't her."

"Gotti, I swear on my life, I never knew that man was messing around with yo' chick. The man just came and dropped twenty-five birds off for me and you. He was by himself. I never see him with anyone. Think about what you're saying. I've never even seen this girl you're speaking on."

No matter how bad he wanted to put a bullet in his cousin's head, he knew his words were the truth. The same nigga he was putting in work for was putting it down between Storm's legs every night. Gotti couldn't believe he was actually shaking hands with the same man who stole his heart away from him.

"Where the fuck that dope at?" He snapped out of his thoughts quickly. Sighing deeply, Clyde pointed to the kitchen. "Bag that shit up, all of it!" he demanded, waving the gun around impatiently.

Clyde stood to his feet, stumbled to the dining table and placed the kilos back into the same duffle he received them in.

"Gotti, you ain't gotta do this cuz. We in this together. How the hell do I explain to this man that his shit gone? I ain't got no bread to replace twenty-five keys, bro."

"Do what you been doing lame ass nigga. Run ya' mouth and tell 'em I got it. I ain't hard to find." He snatched the bag up while backing out of the kitchen.

As he left out of the house, he added another mission to his agenda. Kill Dominic and force Storm to bring her ass back or bury them both next to each other inside the creek.

***

Storm wiped her mouth with the cloth napkin, then placed it beside her empty plate. Dominic had prepared them a lovely lobster dinner with garlic potatoes and salad after they returned from Lennox Mall.

"Oh, my God, baby that food was so good. Thank you."

"You're welcome, baby, and you wanted takeout food."

Dominic pushed his plate away, but his eyes remained on the prize in front of him. His wife was a rare diamond. Life was pointless without her, therefore he made it his mission to shower her with love, affection, and gifts to compensate for what he lacked.

Turning up her fourth glass of wine, Storm finished what was left and casually walked over to her husband. A tingling sensation took over her body, as the effects of the alcohol made a grand appearance.

"I knew there was a reason I married you besides you being so handsome and charming." She leaned down and kissed his lips.

He stroked his beard as he gazed into her eyes. "Well you know, I only married you so I could dig inside this treasure box you kept hidden away for so long."

"Was it worth the wait?"

Dominic's eyes lost focus, as they landed on the motherland. Storm's camel toe was poking through her tights, teasing him. The desire he had for her was strong, which made it harder to keep his hands to himself. Explicit thoughts of him tongue kissing her caused him to lick his own. Gently, he eased his hands between her legs and massaged her kitty, making her weak.

"Hell, yeah, all of this belongs to me and only me. You remember what I told you?"

"Sss—yes, I do baby, it's all yours." Storm loved his frisky behavior and his ability to give her pleasure by his touch alone. Excitement filled her eyes and she bit down on her lip. "Don't start nothing you can't finish sir."

Intense pressure started to build up in his boxers and his stiffening pole pressed hard against the zipper on his pants, threatening to bust it wide open. Quickly, he glanced at his timepiece on his wrist. It was a quarter to nine. Clyde had called him back to back, but he ignored it.

"It's late and I'm busy, so he will have to wait until tomorrow. I have business to handle, right here. So, yeah, I can definitely finish what I'm trying to jump start."

As his hand rested on her waist he tugged at the waistband of her tights and eased them far enough to see the kitty. It was time to make the magic happen right there at the kitchen table for the first time. Eagerly, his thumb made its way between her plump lips and onto her pearl. Storm's eyes rolled to the back of her head as he teased and rubbed her clitoris. There was no way she could resist his touch even if she wanted to.

Storm grabbed Dominic's head, leading him to the well that awaited to quench his thirst. The coldness of his tongue sent shivers down her spine. Unable to move her leg, so he could go deeper, she shimmied out of her pants until they were at her ankles. That didn't interrupt Dominic from feasting because he was latched onto her clit like a newborn on a nipple.

"Yes, baby, suck your pussy." Storm propped her leg between his legs and held onto the back of the chair.

Dominic's erection was getting harder and out of room to extend, so he freed him. "Ride him, baby."

Storm straddled his lap and eased down onto the pole until every inch disappeared, filling her completely. Aggressively, she rocked back and forth and bounced up and down. The gushy, wet sound played out loud like instrumental music. Dominic wrapped his arm around her waist, locked her down and matched her thrusts with hard jabs to the gut.

"Damn, baby, this pussy so warm. Grind hard on yo' dick."

Storm put her arm around his neck and grinded harder. "I love you. I belong to you and only you," she repeated, trying to convince herself that sleeping with Gotti was a mistake.

Dominic raised her shirt and popped one of her savory nipples in his mouth, then started nibbling gently.

"Wait, baby—wait," Storm moaned.

"Nah," he grunted and placed his hand around her throat. "Take all this dick. You was just trying to fuck me like a lil' ass boy a minute ago."

"Stop please," she whined.

"No, bounce on it."

Storm's body stopped moving, as she leaned to the side. A large splash hit the floor causing Dominic to stop stroking. "What the hell was that?"

He looked at Storm, but her face wasn't pleasant and the corners of her mouth had residue on them. Then onto the floor where he saw a puddle of vomit. Storm leaned over again and threw up some more. Dominic held her hair out of her face until she finished.

"Baby, you okay?" he asked while grabbing the cloth napkin from the table to clean her mouth.

"No, I don't feel too good."

"Come on let's get you in the shower."

Dominic carried her to the shower and helped her bathe. Once she was clean, they headed to the bedroom. Storm was dressed in pajamas when he tucked her in and kissed her forehead.

"I'll be right back. I'm going to clean up the mess in the kitchen. If you have to go again use this garbage can."

"Thank you, baby, I'm sorry for ruining the night with all the drinking."

"No need to apologize, baby."

"Okay."

Storm rolled over onto her side and closed her eyes.

Chapter 20

The next day Storm sat at her desk with a horrible migraine. Dominic advised her to stay home, but she decided against it and came into work. Now she regretted every minute of it. She laid her head down on the desk, closed her eyes and waited for the Tylenol to kick in. Minutes passed and a knock on the door interrupted her cat nap.

"Come in!" she shouted.

The door opened and closed, but she didn't bother looking up. Whoever it was wouldn't be there long anyway.

"What's up, chick?"

"Kendra, why are you so loud?" Storm raised her head to see that Kendra had taken a seat across from her.

"Eww! What's wrong with you?"

"I have a headache and I was sick last night."

"So, why did you come to work again?"

"I don't know."

"Mmm." Kendra scrunched up her face. "Bitch, you might be pregnant."

"I seriously doubt that."

"Girl you having sex damn near every night, so it's possible." Kendra stood up and smile. "I'm going to get a pregnancy from the emergency room, I'll be right back."

"You wasting your time." Storm nodded and put her head back on the desk.

Kendra ran around the corner to the emergency and took a test from the cabinet before taking off. On her way back to Storm, she ran all the way there. She was anxious to see if her friend was indeed carrying a child that she so desperately wanted. When she busted back into the office Storm was still in the same spot.

"Get up and let's go to the bathroom." Kendra grabbed her arm just in case her legs grew weak and escorted her to the nearest bathroom.

"I can't believe I let you bring me in here. I'm telling you, I'm not pregnant. Starting a family isn't on Dominic's list of things to do."

"Yeah, yeah, whatever. Pee in this cup so we can see." Kendra forcefully pushed the cup in Storm's hand. "I'll be right here waiting."

"I'm sure you will."

Storm went into the bathroom and closed the stall behind her. Moments later, she returned with a full cup and placed it on the sink.

"That wasn't so hard was it?"

"Painful."

Kendra used the little syringe to place a few drops onto the stick, then set the alarm on her phone for three minutes. Patiently, both ladies waited in silence for the results to come back.

"Are you nervous?" Kendra asked while playing in Storm's hair.

"No, I'm just not in the mood for disappointment. I took a test weeks after the honeymoon and it came back negative. And we had sex every damn night."

"Oh, I didn't know that."

"It wasn't anything to tell, so I kept it to myself. My cycle was late from all of the stress I guess."

"Yeah, that'll do it." Kendra sighed, before changing the subject. "Jade asked about you."

Storm rolled her eyes hard. "Don't tell her nothing about me. Jade is dead to me, so I don't care to hear nothing about her backstabbing ass."

"Don't you think it's been long enough? You throwing away a friendship over some dick that you don't want. You're married now! So, why continue holding this grudge? A nigga gone be a nigga and I don't recall you being this mad with, Gotti."

Storm stood there in silence with a sullen look plastered on her face. "And how would you know that?"

"The fact that you still wanted to fuck him is how I know."

No lies were detected because after the first night she gave in and slept with Gotti, she doubled back a few times in private. She hadn't even told Tia, that she continued to sleep with him. In Storm's defense, she felt like she needed to be there in order to help him cope with the death of his grandma. Gotti's state of mind was in a jumble and she didn't want to see him dead or back in prison.

"I'm not going to respond to that."

"You know I'm right. As women, we can't and won't forgive our friends for one mistake. But we are quick to forgive a man who hurt us, lied and cheated on us. That makes no sense."

The stopwatch on Kendra's cellphone put an end to their little dispute. Storm was nervous, but her gut feeling told her the result was going to be negative. She watched as Kendra picked up the test. The expression on her face was blank, so that was the confirmation to what she already knew.

"See, I told you. Now throw that away and let's get out of this damn bathroom like this is the lunch spot." Storm turned on her heels and headed towards the door.

"Yeah, you right let's go eat because my niece or nephew probably hungry, right now."

All of her movements came to a halt. Slowly, she turned back to face Kendra. "What?"

She held the test up so she could see it. "You're going to be a mommy girl. It's positive!"

"Let me see." Storm beamed, as she rushed in her direction, snatching the test from her hands. The twinkle in her eyes expressed the happiness she felt in her heart. "Wow, I'm pregnant for real! This can't be real." She gasped, placing her hand over her mouth.

"Believe it girl, congratulations!" Kendra hugged her tight. "I'm so happy for you."

"Thanks, Ken, I can't believe this is really happening."

"I told you."

"I need a sonogram, so I'll know for sure."

Kendra released her hold on Storm and smiled. "Shit, let's go to labor and delivery. My homegirl will do it for me."

"I'm so excited."

"As you should be." Finally, they exited the restroom.

***

Standing next to the entrance of his kitchen, Gotti watched the movement of his spot flow like water. Thanks to the new product he received free of charge his status would rise and crush all the other fake ass competition to the ground. Thumbing through the large bills, Trel broke his concentration.

"Yo' Gotti, somebody keep blowing yo' phone up. It's like three missed calls."

Flashing him a bitter look, he shook his head. "Don't you see me counting money? And you should be cutting up dope right?"

"Yeah, but this shit gotta be important. I can't focus if this bitch keep ringing every thirty seconds," he replied holding the cellphone in his palm.

Gotti removed it from his hand and glanced at the screen. Seeing Storm's name caused his attitude to bubble quickly. The thought of her fucking the boss man was on his mind heavy especially after catching her in public with the nigga like he couldn't get touched. The thought of stressing his faults with Jade was enough torment alone but sleeping with a nigga who lived the same lifestyle was like a slap in the face. After calling her numerous times the night before, he decided to return her call.

"Hello?"

"Mighty funny I called your phone last night a million times and you couldn't pick up. I guess you got some free time now that you ain't around yo' hoe ass husband, huh?"

"Excuse me?"

"You fucking heard me," he barked into the receiver. "You got a time limit on when you fuck with me."

A moment of silence crept through the line before she spoke. "Gotti, you know I'm married. It's not a secret. I've tried to be considerate to your feelings knowing that you just lost your grandmother including me not wanting to see you end back up in a bad position for thinking irrational. So, yes, I have enough respect for my husband not to answer the phone for you."

Gotti turned his back to the workers and cuffed the phone up to his mouth. "But I guess you ain't got enough respect for him to stop fucking me like I got a good chance of getting back together with you tho'?"

"You knew there was never a chance. You slept with my best friend and crossed a line that's unforgivable, Gotti! This is something you just have to accept. It's already too much and I'm not about to destroy my family because of something that's not meant to be. Please just move on."

"Don't you get this shit? There is no damn family if it ain't with me, Storm. It's no such thing as walking out of nothing. You running around with a nigga I do business with. A nigga I've been so close to that I could've snatched his head off in a second. Now you get this through your thick ass skull. If I can't have you, nobody can. You must think you the only person who shops at Lennox. I could've done some terrible shit and popped that boy's brain loose in front of ya' face. Instead, I wanted to offer you another chance to stand by my side again. To let the past rest and understand that we all make mistakes."

"I don't care if you have your little friend Jade following me or whatever. It's not gonna work, Gotti. I'm going to be with my husband and live my life. You have to remember that you're out on parole. You wouldn't wanna mess that up. You'll be back behind a wall if you come anywhere near me or my man. I'm sorry but what we had is over. Goodbye Gotti!"

Hearing the line click caused him to pause and punch the wall in front of him. Trel could see the fire that burned in his pupils and decided to excuse himself. Storm's words would be the reason for another door closing on his heart. Sparing anyone from that point on was out of the question. Boundaries were about to be eliminated and she would be the first person to receive the example on why not to play with a cold heart.

* * *

As he sat at home inside of his office, Dominic leaned back with a smile after closing the new large deal on the car dealership. The extra money would set them straight for the rest of their lives and it was all complete. Hopefully, after telling Storm a few big tickets were in the account she would actually consider quitting and embrace the pampering he was so ready to give.

The vibration of his cell captured his attention. Checking the number, he viewed Clyde's name and answered on the third ring.

"Ain't no way you've called me nine times since last night? Is it already that time?"

"I been trying my best to get in contact with you, D. We got a problem," Clyde responded in a feeble tone.

Wrinkling his eyebrow, Dominic sat up straight. "We don't have problems. Success is all I know so what are you talking about?"

"My cousin, he came to the house yesterday on a rampage about a bitch. We got into a fight and he robbed me for the work."

"You let Max take my shit! What the fuck do y'all idiots drama got to do with me. I'm guessing you're about to straighten that and cough up my two hundred and fifty grand. Correct?" His voice boomed sternly.

"Bossman the drama wasn't between us. His beef is with you. He came over stressing about you running around the city with his girl. He said that I had to know about it because I worked for you."

"I'm afraid he's gotten me mixed up with another clown from his neighborhood. I got a wife, not a hooker. I can guarantee that she doesn't know, Max."

"His name is, Gotti not Max," Clyde admitted.

"What?"

"My cousin's name is, Gotti. He lied about his name because he wanted to stay under the radar after making it home. I had nothing to do with this. I don't even know what the fuck is going on."

The day he shared lunch with Jade instantly struck his mind. "You brought this nigga to me about doing business and knew he was hiding something? You've placed my family and my entire operation in jeopardy, and you tell me this after this man runs off with all my property."

"I would never bring any bad business your way. I know how you move about your money. This wasn't no shit I intended to happen, bro. I wouldn't be sitting here talking on the other end of this phone if it was some type of game. He said the beef was with you and that he ain't hard to find."

Dominic rubbed a hand through his waves and loosened his shirt collar. "I'ma break you in on a little news, Clyde. The truth always happens to find its way to the surface. I provide for my wife, myself and of course the ones on my payroll. I don't take losses. Period! I'm gonna give you three days to call the kid and explain that he's making a deadly mistake. Because if I can't get it back that debt falls on you and so does his blood. Take it easy, I'll be expecting your call," Dominic stated before ending the conversation.

Soaking in what he was just told had his mind spinning. Not letting someone that close to pull a stunt was his number one rule and it was finally broken. Even worse was hearing that Storm's past was the reason. He stood up out of his chair and moved to the window just as her car pulled into the driveway.

Destiny Skai & Chris Green

Chapter 21

Ever since Storm left the hospital she couldn't stop staring at the sonogram. That was the best news she'd received. Nothing or no one was going to ruin her moment. Not even the threats from Gotti's mentally unstable ass. All she wanted was to be a mother and the time had finally presented itself. Now, she could finally quit her job and be the housewife Dominic wanted her to be. Silencing the engine, she grabbed her belongings and stepped from the vehicle.

"I hope he's excited." She grinned from ear to ear.

The fact that Dominic wasn't pressed about having babies made her a little uncertain about the way to break the news to him. After the planning and plotting, she'd finally got her baby. Dominic had no clue that she'd been taking birth control pills or tracking her cycle in an effort to get pregnant. Nor was he going to find out.

Storm opened up the door and walked inside. The house was quiet as usual and Dominic was nowhere in sight. "Dominic," she called out. "Where are you, baby?"

She went from room to room until he answered. "I'm in my office."

When Storm stepped foot inside, Dominic was sitting at his desk with his eyes closed and fingers resting on his forehead. "Hey, baby, how was your day?"

Dominic opened his eyes and looked directly into hers. Everything he'd heard before her arrival wasn't sitting too well with him. "Interesting and very long."

"I see, you look stressed." Sitting her things on his desk, Storm walked over to him and placed her hands on his shoulders.

"A little, but it's nothing that can't be fixed."

As she massaged his broad shoulders, she could feel that he was tense. "Relax baby, I'm here to relieve all of your stress."

"Why are you in such a good mood?" he questioned.

"Well." She grinned. "I have some good news for you."

Dominic paused for a moment before replying. "And what's that?"

"I put in my two-week notice today."

He reached up and grabbed her hands. "It's about time, baby. But why the sudden change?"

Storm could no longer contain her happiness, so she stood in front of him with the biggest smile on her face. "Are you ready?"

The crease in his brow shifted downward. "As ready as I'm going to be."

"Well, do you remember when I said there was only one way, I would quit my job and become a stay at home wife?"

"Vaguely," he replied impatiently waiting on her surprise.

"Baby, I'm pregnant." Storm grabbed his hands and placed them on her stomach. "We're going to have a baby."

Dominic had a perplexed look on his face. "Huh, what do you mean?"

"I was just as confused as you and I didn't expect it. But I took a test today and it came back positive." Filled with so much excitement, she reached for her bag and pulled out the sonogram. "It's really happening, baby. You said to have patience and it would happen."

Dominic took the sonogram from her hands and stared at it. His words were unable to escape his mouth as he observed the small life on the picture in front of him. Just as he lifted up his head to speak, he was cut off from the vibration of his cell. Without looking to see who it was he answered.

"Hello?"

"If it ain't, Mr. Captain Save A Bitch himself. I see you have a problem answering the phone also."

Smirking at Storm, he leaned back in his chair. "Max?"

"Gotti, bitch nigga, get that shit right. I actually thought you could've been a cool older cat to soak up some game from. But you turned out to be lamer than I expected. If you don't mind, I need you to put Storm on the phone because she ain't picking up."

"You got some big nuts calling my line after pulling that stunt with, Clyde. Maybe I didn't make myself clear enough when we first met, little boy. I'm a man of business and playing with my money is something I don't take lightly. My wife is also added in that equation. If you have any plans on enjoying your life in the near future. I would suggest you return what's mine and hang yourself off the nearest bridge," Dominic stated while staring into Storm's eyes.

"And you must of forgot what I explained to yo' bitch ass when we met. I don't just go for anything. I think you're confused, Superman. All your work—I mean my work is doing numbers in the spot, right now. That's a dead issue so we can kill that conversation. The only thing you need to hand over now is, my bitch. See you're confusing her. She only thinks she needs you, but she loves me."

"I think you've been smoking on that supply lil' nigga. My lady doesn't want you. Why would she settle for a coach plane ticket when I can purchase her the whole airport? You're trying to play a game that you can't win."

Laughing loudly into the receiver, Gotti yawned. "Is that right? I think I've already won. See, while you was at home with the apron on cooking casserole for dinner. I was digging a tunnel in that pussy. She was so wet that she damn near drowned me. I'm talking fresh out the chain-gang pussy." Dominic bit down on his bottom lip to hold his composure as Gotti continued to rant. "She's not the woman for you. You're more of a fake ass, Morris Chestnut type nigga. All soft and cuddly, Storm, is used to men like me. Thorough, a gangsta by heart. Beef is something I don't do, especially about a woman who belongs to me. So, I'll make a deal with you. Leave my bitch alone and take your loss. Tell her that you made a mistake with the marriage and you're deeply sorry for wasting her time. She'll come back to me and you will leave town and never return. If you agree, I will spare you on the bullshit I'm ready to release. We all know how Juve ended up."

"For some reason, it's always a stupid young jackass like you to make a boss like me step out of my character. How about this, I'll give you a chance to bring my shit back. Not half, every fuckin' crumb. Then I'll give you the decision on where you would like to be buried. There's plenty of cemeteries around Atlanta. All you have to do is pick one."

"True, but as long as you and her, are buried next to me I wouldn't give a fuck. Clean out your ears old man, I don't have nothing to lose. I don't care who gets hurt. It doesn't matter where you go or who you call. I won't stop until I have her back," Gotti warned with surety lacing his tone.

Feeling the anger pour from Dominic's skin, Storm grew nervous. "Baby, who are you talking to?"

Shaking his head in a disappointed manner, he raised a finger to silence her.

"Look, dude, the only thing you're gonna bury is your head inside another powder sack because you're talking crazy. I make a living off being organized and humble. So, I'll excuse the stupid insults. Nothing in this world can be so addictive for a man to not let go. You're more of a stalker. A leech that can't accept being alone. It hurts you to see her win, doesn't it? To see that you messed up and lost everything you thought was yours. Unfortunately, the time for trying is too late. You're a fucking coward and the only thing you're good for is beating yo' bunkmate dick. Is that why you don't care about nothing? Because you wanna make it back to prison to greet your real lover. Do yourself a favor and take heed to what I'm saying. Pay me for my shit and split before I part yo' bitch ass like the red sea."

"I see that this is getting nowhere, and I refuse to waste another second hearing you cry like a hoe. Since you wanna play this tough guy game. The war is on, I hope you got a bulletproof vest to protect your head, fuck nigga," Gotti threatened before hanging up.

"Dominic who was that?" Storm asked feeling the heated tension.

Dominic exhaled and looked into her eyes. "That was, Gotti."

The circulation in her body felt as if it had stopped after hearing his name. Storm stuttered trying to find a reply, as Dominic placed the phone in front of him.

"Sit yo' ass down," he demanded with a stern voice.

Easing into the seat in front of her, she lowered her vision as he scooted closer. "I think it's time for you to tell me what's really going on."

Feeling the tears fill her eyes, she matched his gaze.

To Be continued…
Marred to a Boss, Pregnant by my Ex 2
Coming Soon

Submission Guideline

Submit the first three chapters of your completed manuscript to ldpsubmissions@gmail.com, subject line: Your book's title. The manuscript must be in a .doc file and sent as an attachment. Document should be in Times New Roman, double spaced and in size 12 font. Also, provide your synopsis and full contact information. If sending multiple submissions, they must each be in a separate email.

Have a story but no way to send it electronically? You can still submit to LDP/Ca$h Presents. Send in the first three chapters, written or typed, of your completed manuscript to:

LDP: Submissions Dept
Po Box 870494
Mesquite, Tx 75187

DO NOT send original manuscript. Must be a duplicate.

Provide your synopsis and a cover letter containing your full contact information.

Thanks for considering LDP and Ca$h Presents.

Married to a Boss, Pregnant by my Ex

Coming Soon from Lock Down Publications/Ca$h Presents

BOW DOWN TO MY GANGSTA

By **Ca$h**

TORN BETWEEN TWO

By **Coffee**

BLOOD STAINS OF A SHOTTA **III**

By **Jamaica**

STEADY MOBBIN **III**

By **Marcellus Allen**

BLOOD OF A BOSS **V**

By **Askari**

LOYAL TO THE GAME **IV**

LIFE OF SIN II

By **T.J. & Jelissa**

A DOPEBOY'S PRAYER **II**

By **Eddie "Wolf" Lee**

IF LOVING YOU IS WRONG… **III**

LOVE ME EVEN WHEN IT HURTS **II**

By **Jelissa**

TRUE SAVAGE **VI**

By **Chris Green**

BLAST FOR ME **III**

A BRONX TALE III

DUFFLE BAG CARTEL

By **Ghost**

ADDICTIED TO THE DRAMA **III**

By **Jamila Mathis**

LIPSTICK KILLAH **III**

WHAT BAD BITCHES DO **III**

KILL ZONE **II**

By **Aryanna**

THE COST OF LOYALTY **II**

By **Kweli**

SHE FELL IN LOVE WITH A REAL ONE **II**

By **Tamara Butler**

LOVE SHOULDN'T HURT **III**

RENEGADE BOYS **III**

By **Meesha**

CORRUPTED BY A GANGSTA **IV**

By **Destiny Skai**

A GANGSTER'S CODE **III**

By **J-Blunt**

KING OF NEW YORK IV

RISE TO POWER II

By **T.J. Edwards**

GORILLAS IN THE BAY II

De'Kari

THE STREETS ARE CALLING II

Duquie Wilson

KINGPIN KILLAZ III

Hood Rich

STEADY MOBBIN' **III**

Marcellus Allen

SINS OF A HUSTLA II

ASAD

CASH MONEY HOES

Nicole Goosby

TRIGGADALE II

Elijah R. Freeman

MARRIED TO A BOSS 2...

By Destiny Skai & Chris Green

Available Now

RESTRAINING ORDER **I & II**

By **CA$H & Coffee**

LOVE KNOWS NO BOUNDARIES **I II & III**

By **Coffee**

RAISED AS A GOON I, II, III & IV

BRED BY THE SLUMS I, II, III

BLAST FOR ME I & II

ROTTEN TO THE CORE I III

A BRONX TALE I, II

By **Ghost**

LAY IT DOWN **I & II**

LAST OF A DYING BREED

BLOOD STAINS OF A SHOTTA I & II

By **Jamaica**

LOYAL TO THE GAME

LOYAL TO THE GAME II

LOYAL TO THE GAME III

LIFE OF SIN

By **TJ & Jelissa**

BLOODY COMMAS I & II

SKI MASK CARTEL I II & III

KING OF NEW YORK I II,III

RISE TO POWER

By **T.J. Edwards**

IF LOVING HIM IS WRONG...I & II

LOVE ME EVEN WHEN IT HURTS

By **Jelissa**

WHEN THE STREETS CLAP BACK I & II III

By **Jibril Williams**

A DISTINGUISHED THUG STOLE MY HEART I II & III

LOVE SHOULDN'T HURT I II

RENEGADE BOYS I & II

By **Meesha**

A GANGSTER'S CODE I & II

By **J-Blunt**

PUSH IT TO THE LIMIT

By **Bre' Hayes**

BLOOD OF A BOSS **I, II, III & IV**

By **Askari**

THE STREETS BLEED MURDER **I, II & III**

THE HEART OF A GANGSTA I II& III

By **Jerry Jackson**

CUM FOR ME

CUM FOR ME 2

CUM FOR ME 3

CUM FOR ME 4

An **LDP Erotica Collaboration**

BRIDE OF A HUSTLA **I II & II**

THE FETTI GIRLS **I, II& III**

CORRUPTED BY A GANGSTA I, II & III

Married to a Boss, Pregnant by my Ex

By **Destiny Skai**
WHEN A GOOD GIRL GOES BAD
By **Adrienne**
A GANGSTER'S REVENGE **I II III & IV**
THE BOSS MAN'S DAUGHTERS
THE BOSS MAN'S DAUGHTERS II
THE BOSSMAN'S DAUGHTERS III
THE BOSSMAN'S DAUGHTERS IV
THE BOSS MAN'S DAUGHTERS **V**
A SAVAGE LOVE **I & II**
BAE BELONGS TO ME
A HUSTLER'S DECEIT I, II
WHAT BAD BITCHES DO I, II
By **Aryanna**
A KINGPIN'S AMBITON
A KINGPIN'S AMBITION **II**
I MURDER FOR THE DOUGH
By **Ambitious**
TRUE SAVAGE
TRUE SAVAGE II
TRUE SAVAGE **III**
TRUE SAVAGE **IV**
TRUE SAVAGE **V**
By **Chris Green**
A DOPEBOY'S PRAYER
By **Eddie "Wolf" Lee**
THE KING CARTEL **I, II & III**
By **Frank Gresham**
THESE NIGGAS AIN'T LOYAL **I, II & III**

163

By **Nikki Tee**
GANGSTA SHYT **I II &III**
By **CATO**
THE ULTIMATE BETRAYAL
By **Phoenix**
BOSS'N UP **I , II & III**
By **Royal Nicole**
I LOVE YOU TO DEATH
By Destiny J
I RIDE FOR MY HITTA
I STILL RIDE FOR MY HITTA
By **Misty Holt**
LOVE & CHASIN' PAPER
By **Qay Crockett**
TO DIE IN VAIN
SINS OF A HUSTLA
By **ASAD**
BROOKLYN HUSTLAZ
By **Boogsy Morina**
BROOKLYN ON LOCK I & II
By **Sonovia**
GANGSTA CITY
By **Teddy Duke**
A DRUG KING AND HIS DIAMOND I & II III
A DOPEMAN'S RICHES
HER MAN, MINE'S TOO I, II
By Nicole Goosby
TRAPHOUSE KING **I II & III**
KINGPIN KILLAZ

By **Hood Rich**

LIPSTICK KILLAH **I, II**

CRIME OF PASSION I & II

By **Mimi**

STEADY MOBBN' **I, II**

By **Marcellus Allen**

WHO SHOT YA **I, II**

Renta

GORILLAZ IN THE BAY

DE'KARI

TRIGGADALE

Elijah R. Freeman

GOD BLESS THE TRAPPERS I, II, III

THESE SCANDALOUS STREETS I, II, III

FEAR MY GANGSTA I, II, III

THESE STREETS DON'T LOVE NOBODY I, II

Tranay Adams

THE STREETS ARE CALLING

Duquie Wilson

MARRIED TO A BOSS…

By Destiny Skai & Chris Green

BOOKS BY LDP'S CEO, CA$H

TRUST IN NO MAN

TRUST IN NO MAN 2

TRUST IN NO MAN 3

BONDED BY BLOOD

SHORTY GOT A THUG

THUGS CRY

THUGS CRY 2

THUGS CRY 3

TRUST NO BITCH

TRUST NO BITCH 2

TRUST NO BITCH 3

TIL MY CASKET DROPS

RESTRAINING ORDER

RESTRAINING ORDER 2

IN LOVE WITH A CONVICT

Coming Soon

BONDED BY BLOOD 2

BOW DOWN TO MY GANGSTA

CPSIA information can be obtained
at www.ICGtesting.com
Printed in the USA
LVHW080200090719
623528LV00014B/139/P